"Just get away from me. Get the hell away from me!"

I never saw the punch. The side of my jaw blew up and, after a curious interlude of weightlessness, I landed flat on my back in the water below the dock.

I swam to where I could walk, and I walked ashore. He was waiting for me. He came in and hooked me three times on the jaw and once in the stomach and I clubbed him hard. He came in again, and it was the same sort of thing, but I hit him a little bit better. I didn't think about the pain or the blood in my mouth or the people watching me. I thought about staying on my feet and getting that one solid blow.

"Fall ... damn you Fall!" he said, and I knew he was winded. ...

Fawcett Gold Medal Books
by John D. MacDonald:

TRAVIS McGEE SERIES

JOHN D. MacDONALD

A
MAN
OF
AFFAIRS

FAWCETT GOLD MEDAL • NEW YORK

A Fawcett Gold Medal Book
Published by Ballantine Books
Copyright © 1957 by John D. MacDonald Publishing, Inc.

ISBN 0-449-12966-6

Manufactured in the United States of America

First Fawcett Gold Medal Edition: July 1965
First Ballantine Books Edition: February 1984
Second Printing: January 1986

ONE

I GOT OUT OF MY CAR and stood beside it on the gravel driveway and looked at the big frame house. I had not seen it in over two years, not since the death of Louise's father put an end to those futile and meaningless conferences he used to hold in his home. The house and grounds had not changed. The blinds were closed against the heat of a midmorning Monday in May. The plantings were as formal and rich and well-tended as ever.

I tried to calm myself with a cigarette. It would do no good to rush in full of anger and indignation and confront Louise. Louise had too much experience with being bullied. Just a half hour earlier I had dropped into the bank to see Walt Burgeson, and he had been very uncomfortable as he had told me the sorry and disappointing news about Louise's unexpected decision—the decision that might well spill all the apples out of our basket.

Though I had seen Louise here and there during the two years since her father's death, I'd had no close contact with her. Louise had been off with War- ren Dodge on a honeymoon in Italy when her father, Thomas McGann, met his tragic, slapstick death, a death that must have infuriated him during his final microsecond of awareness. The way it was recon- structed, he had dropped the soap and it had bounded out of the shower stall. When he stepped out he stepped directly onto it, and in falling struck his head squarely and irrevocably on the porcelained rim of the toilet. He had been a big and ponderous man, muscled like a steer.

5

I had a clear memory of how Louise and Warren Dodge had looked at the time of the funeral, after their flying trip home from Italy—Warren big and beefy, solemn and sullen, heavily scented with bonded whisky—Louise remote and subdued and pallid, more spiritless than even the death of her father would have seemed to warrant.

There are only seventy thousand people in Portston and so I had seen her around fairly often during the two years. And thought she looked unhappy. And heard the unsavory rumors about her marriage. I didn't need the rumors. I knew what sort of man she had married.

I snapped the cigarette away, went to the door and pushed the bell. The door opened and a heavy Negro woman looked at me quite blankly. "I'd like to see Mrs. Dodge, please."

"She busy now."

"Go tell her Sam Glidden wants to see her right now!"

Some of my urgency and anger must have been apparent. I'm big and I've been told by intimates that I look a good deal rougher and tougher than I am. I saw a wider stripe of the whites of her eyes as she closed the door. She was back in a minute and a half to say, "She says you come back in the garden."

I followed her through the house. There were glints of polish on the dark and heavy furniture, discreet gleams of brass and silver, a scent of cedar and wax and furniture oils. The house had a hushed feeling, a secret flavor.

The small walled garden behind the house was sunny and bright with flowers. Louise got up from an aluminum chaise longue webbed with white plastic and took my hand and smiled her careful smile and said, "A long time, Sam. Too long."

"It's good to see you, Louise."

She indicated a chair for me and sat back on the chaise longue, still smiling. But I sensed she knew well why I had come. "Beer or anything, Sam?"

"Thanks, no." I had to put her off balance a little bit. She was braced for argumentation. I offered her a cigarette and said, "I was remembering about once upon a time, Louise. The time when I was so in love with you I couldn't even eat."

Her greeny-gray eyes went round-wide with surprise. "Good Lord! When?"

"I was a senior in high, and you were a sophomore. You wore your hair a funny way. Braided and it went across here."

"My coronet braid."

"And you had a blue dress with white at the collar and white on the sleeves."

"I haven't remembered that dress for years. It was a favorite."

"I suffered in silence. Sam Glidden had no business trying to get chummy with the McGann girl. We all knew your father sent you and your brother to public high school because he thought it was the democratic thing to do. Your brother had his own car, and you had your own crowd you ran around with, and as soon as the weather was warm enough you'd all go right from school to the country club to swim and play tennis."

She laughed aloud and it made me feel slightly hurt. "What's so funny?"

"Not what you think, Sam. Right about that time I had a grim little crush on you. But you were unattainable. Big popular senior, football hero. Big Sam Glidden wasn't going to waste any of his time on a sappy little sophomore."

"We should have found out about that," I said. She looked at me and after a few seconds her smile looked as though it had been pasted on, and then she looked away. I knew she was about to ask me why I had come to see her, so I beat her to the gun and said, "I'll never forget how much I owe your father, Louise."

"He was . . . glad he could help you, Sam."

I had worked at the Harrison Corporation plant—Thomas McGann, President—every summer while I was in high school. In my senior year I had a choice of football scholarships; but in the final high school game, I got hit and the cartilage of my right knee was badly torn. The word got around the conference I would be out of the game for two years at least. A football scholarship had been my only prayer of getting to college in spite of reasonably respectable marks. That was 1946 and I was nineteen. I'd been too young for World War II, and the bum knee kept me out of Korea later.

I applied for a job at Harrison, thinking I would save money for a year and then try college the following fall. I didn't know that Thomas McGann was aware of my existence. When I applied for a job in June I got it immediately on the basis of my past working record with them, and three days later I was called out of the shop and sent up to Mr. McGann's office. I soon found he'd followed my football career as well as my record with the company on summer jobs. And he knew my home situation. I was the only child of my mother's first marriage. It had not been a good marriage. When I was eleven, after her fifth year of widowhood, she had married again, married a man she loved, a man who adored her. And there were, by that time, four half-brothers and half-sisters from that second marriage. It was a happy house without much money and without too much emotional room for me.

Mr. McGann offered a deal. He would get me into a good college of business administration and back me for what I needed through four years if I would agree to come back and work for the Harrison Corporation. When I was on salary I could start paying him back.

It took a long time for him to get it through my proud, thick head that it wasn't charity. I took him up on it. When I was twenty-three I came back to work as assistant to the purchasing agent. Five years ago, when I was twenty-five, I paid him back the last dime.

In view of what he had done for me, I had to choose my words carefully in talking to Louise. "I'm grateful to your father, Louise, but that doesn't alter my objective opinion of him. He was an overbearing, strong-minded, stupid man who refused all advice, good or bad, a man who came dangerously close to running a sound company into the ground."

She stared at me for long seconds. She looked very lovely. She was wearing crisp white shorts with a red stripe down the sides, a red halter, red straw slippers. Her black and glossy hair was tied back with a white ribbon. She is not quite tall, and her bone structure is fragile and fine. Her flawless skin has a dusky, honeyed quality, and her legs are smooth and round and long. There is a look of brooding sensitivity about her face. I remembered how she was as a child, full of a dancing and endless vitality, a flame in shades of black and ivory. Now, in her, it is all muted. All fires are banked. But her new quietness does not give the impression of frigidity or sterility. At twenty-seven she has a way about her that is so much more provocative to me than any strip act that I could feel the annoying pulse-thud of awareness of her even while I was trying to make her understand what I had to tell her.

"You'd better explain that to me, Sam," she said quietly.

"He insisted on surrounding himself with yes-men, in making it a one-man operation."

"Then why have you stayed?"

"Because I gave him my promise. I have to tell you something that sounds like I'm giving myself medals, Louise. I'm considered very very good in the field. I've been scouted, and I have had some very handsome offers from some very sound businesses. I'm apparently one of those so-called bright young men that industry can't find enough of. I can't put my finger on what the special talent is. Maybe it's just a combination of being able to think clearly, handle people and work hard. I stayed because I gave my promise."

"I haven't got a good head for business, Sam. But it seems to me that ever since my father died, you and Mr. Dolson have been the ones who have been running the company into the ground. Warren thinks so, too. Look at it from my point of view. My brother Tommy and I each inherited fifty thousand shares of Harrison Common from Grandfather McGann's estate when we were twenty-one. While my father was running the company it was always listed at right around thirty dollars a share, and it always paid a dividend of around two dollars or a little less."

"I know that."

"Tommy and I agreed to vote our shares for the same board and everything, and what happened? There hasn't been a dividend since my father died, and now the stock is listed at twelve dollars."

"Maybe you don't understand the situation because nobody has been blunt enough about your father. Harrison has gradually been losing its competitive position for the last fifteen years. Management has been unaggressive and unrealistic. Not enough money has gone into modernization of plant and equipment, so production costs have been going up in relation to the other firms in the industry. So profits have been going down. The distribution system is antiquated and inefficient. We aren't getting our fair share of the market. There was no reason to maintain that dividend rate. Your father was paying out in dividends money that should have been used for modernization. It was like . . . with a car, buying a quart of oil every ten miles instead of paying for a ring job. Louise, we've got to work like dogs to catch up. We *had* to pass the dividends. We've got to modernize and cut production costs, or we're sunk."

"How long will it take?" she asked me.

I shrugged. "The way it looks it should be another two or three years before we can start paying
legitimate dividends. Then they'll only amount to maybe two bits a share. But by then we should be getting
healthy."

"If things are as horrible as you say, then why is
Mike Dean interested in the company?"

"Mike Dean is not interested in the company, Louise. Mike Dean is interested in making some money for
Mike Dean. He doesn't care if he sinks us without a
trace."

"Are you trying to frighten me?"

I despaired of trying to make her understand about
Mike Dean. Mike Dean is a member of a small group
of men who have come into curious prominence in the
past few years. You see their pictures in *Business
Week* and *Fortune* and *Time*. "This week, Mike Dean,
suave and unscarred veteran of bitter proxy battles
and corporate infighting, accused the management
of the XYQ Company of a stale and unrealistic approach to the pressing problems of the industry."
Mike is always termed controversial, or a man of
mystery. His thick thumb is in dozens of pies. He
operates from a confusing web of interrelated corporate setups and has surrounded himself with a
knife-sharp staff of C.P.A.'s, tax attorneys, engineers
and management specialists.

The Mike Deans operate in the rich realm of capital
gains. And they gain a spurious rectitude by cutting
figures in the public eye in on the pies they bake.

I tried to explain it to Louise as simply as I could.
"Mike Dean has people who spend their time reading
balance sheets, Louise. They look for one special cir-
cumstance. They look for a company like Harrison,
where the book value of the stock is higher than the
market value. When we passed the dividends, we left
ourselves open to an operator like Dean. The stock was
selling at eleven or twelve. Try to follow me, now.
Please. That means that with four hundred and forty

thousand shares of stock outstanding, the company was valued in the market place at four million, eight hundred and forty thousand dollars. Yet, if we closed up shop tomorrow, liquidated everything, equipment, buildings, reserves, inventory, accounts receivable, we could realize a total of nearly nine million. That means our book value is twenty dollars a share. The differential is what brought Mike down on us like a wolf on the fold. We know that he started over a year ago buying Harrison Common very, very cautiously so as not to attract attention or force the price up. Three months ago he came out in the open and started his campaign to get proxies. We can estimate that he and his group own or control close to one hundred and ninety thousand shares of Harrison voting stock. When we have the Board meeting on the first of June, he can force representation on the Board of Directors, but he cannot take control. Let's suppose he could take control. By a change in the dividend policy, and by liquidating some of the Harrison assets, he might be able to push the stock up to thirty-five or even forty. Then he could unload for a long-term capital gain, go over on the short side and ride the stock right back down into the ground. Say he personally holds one hundred thousand shares. I can see how he could make a profit of thirty dollars a share. And pay only a twenty-six per cent tax on his three million gain."

She nibbled at her thumb knuckle. "How do you know he doesn't want to do what you're trying to do? I mean modernize and so on."

"That's what he's announced he wants to do, naturally. But will he do that? Or is this just a raid? We thought we were safe, Louise. We didn't know that you and Tommy might go back on your promise to Al Dolson. We thought the hundred thousand shares would be voted our way. Those shares are our margin of safety. But this morning Walt Burgeson at the bank phoned me at the office and asked me to come in as soon as I could. He told me what you're planning to do."

She gave me a furious look. "You make it sound as if we're being sneaky. All this talk about going back on promises."

"Now wait a minute."

"You wait a minute, Sam Glidden. A very nice man named Fletcher Bowman was in town last week. He took Tommy and me to lunch. He works for Mike Dean. He explained that in all fairness Mr. Dean should be given a chance to explain his position to us because we are the two largest single shareholders and so we have the largest stake in what he's trying to do. That seemed fair to us. We agreed. So, in Mike's name, he invited the four of us—Tommy and Puss, and Warren and me—down to Mr. Dean's place in the Bahamas. A private plane is going to pick us up Wednesday morning. Because we're going down there doesn't mean that we plan to betray anybody. Anyway, I'm curious about him and I'd like to meet him. And it will be a nice vacation."

"I've heard about that hideout of his," I said.

"We're going."

"Understand, Louise, I'm not trying to low rate your intelligence, or Tommy's or anybody else's. This kind of a deal is outside your experience. You're getting mixed up in a very smooth operation. It'll be a big snow job. Then suppose you and Tommy sign proxy forms down there and everything is just dandy."

She got up quickly and walked away from me. She went over near the wall and sat on her heels and began picking dead leaves off a low bush.

"Suppose we do sign them? Suppose he does wreck the company?"

I went over and stood behind her. "What does that mean?"

She stood up and faced me, looking up at me. "Just suppose I don't give a damn any longer? Do

you think I'm happy here? Do you think I look back
on a madly gay childhood? Do you think I'm having
a real dandy marriage? There's enough income from
the things my father left to keep this house up and
live here. If the dividends were still coming in, we
wouldn't be here. So I sound like a spoiled brat.
I'm still trying to make a marriage work. And it doesn't
work well at all here in Portston. I can tell you that
much. So suppose he does take over. The stock will
go up, won't it? He'll make it go up. And then I
can sell the damn stuff and get away from here for
keeps." And she turned abruptly to hide tears and
began picking off the dead leaves again.

"Let me be corny for a minute, Louise."

"Go right ahead," she said in a muffled voice.

"In 1858 your great-great-grandfather, Aaron Harrison, started the company. His only daughter, Jessica,
married the first Tom McGann. They were a rugged
pair, Aaron and Tom. They built this house."

"No. It was his son."

"At any rate, they felt their obligations to the company and to the community. They bulled their way
through panics and depressions. They had maybe
too paternalistic an attitude toward labor, but they did
the best they could in the tough times. When your
father took over he had as much strength and power
as the earlier ones, but he lacked their shrewdness.
And he had just as much a feeling of responsibility as
anyone in the past. Your brother is a great guy; but
he couldn't run a hot dog stand, as you well know.
Maybe I'm simple, but to me a company like this is
more than something you make money with. It sup-
ports directly or indirectly a couple of thousand
families and a way of life that doesn't seem too bad
to me. If Dean *should* wreck the firm, he also wrecks
the town. But, naturally, you won't have to give a
damn about that. You'll be living in Amalfi or
Cuernavaca or Malaga."

She turned to look up at me over her shoulder.

"Very touching," she said, but her eyes were still shiny with tears.

"I don't think you ought to go."

"It's all arranged."

I could see all of our planning shot to hell. I could see Al Dolson throwing in the sponge. When Thomas McGann died, Al had been vice-president, and I had been his assistant. He was a mild man in his late fifties. Maybe once upon a time he had some push; but too many years of McGann had driven him back into a polite shell. When the Board, with Walt Burgeson as chairman, had made Al Dolson president, they had made me vice-president. Some of the other men felt that I had been jumped over their heads, that I was too young, and my ideas were too wild; but I had been able to kill off the resentment and get them all pulling together.

I felt as if I were propping Al Dolson up. He was too hesitant about using the authority he held. When we first learned that Mike Dean was snapping at our heels, Al was all set to give up. But I had managed to get him back on the rails. Right after McGann had died we had been in a tunnel where we couldn't see light ahead. But in the last year we had rounded a bend and you could begin to see a far-off glimmer. There was a new bounce and confidence to management. I managed to get Al feeling as I did: that even if Dean did place some people on the Board of Directors, we'd still have enough backing to go ahead in our own way.

But if he felt that the McGann kids were going to sell us out to Dean, thus giving him control of close to seventy per cent of the voting shares, Dolson would fold in on himself like a tissue paper tent. I felt that in a few years he would be all right. He's bright enough, and he's gaining confidence. But this was happening too soon.

I knew that Louise had enough of the McGann stubbornness in her so that I couldn't get her to change her mind. And perhaps she felt it would help her marriage to get away for a while with her husband. I had heard that Warren Dodge did more than his share of tomcatting since they'd moved back to Portston. It's too small a city for much of that.

I could think of only one answer. I checked over what I had lined up to do in the next week. By working like hell the rest of today and all of tomorrow I could get it fairly well cleaned up.

"Okay, so you're going, Louise. But let's say you ought to have somebody around in case you have to ask some questions. Would you object if I went along, too?"

She stood up and she looked agitated. "No, but . . . but you're not invited."

"You could fix that with a phone call, I think. Call the man. Bowden?"

"Bowman. Fletcher Bowman. I have his New York number, yes. But . . ."

"Louise, this is not a social occasion. I am not crashing a party. If you suggest I come along they're going to have to say yes, because they can't afford the impression they'd make by saying no."

Though I wanted to ask to listen on an extension, I waited in the garden. I picked up the book she had been reading and glanced at some of the pages in the middle. A Faulkner novel covering the further adventures of the Snopes family. I wished for more time to read, more time to be by myself. The last two and a half years had been full of furious activity that, at times, had seemed meaningless. The past week I had spent two days out on the coast with Gene Budler—our sales manager—and Cary Murchison of engineering. Gene and I had to explain the new distribution setup to the western wholesalers. We planned to use it as a test area. They were enthusiastic about it. And then Cary Murchison and I spent the rest of the time poking around in some warehouses full of machine tools recently declared surplus by Army

Ordnance. We found a lot of stuff we could use, had a public stenographer type our bids and left them with the military along with a certified check for two hundred and twenty-one thousand dollars.

Every week had been patch and pray, trying to remedy the neglect of two decades and at the same time build soundly for the future. The two most pressing problems coming up were to get some aggressive styling for the new lines, and do battle with the union about work standards.

Louise came back out into the garden. "He acted as if he didn't quite know how to take it at first, and then he got very jolly and said, 'Of course, of course. Do bring Mr. Glidden along.'"

"Those boys don't move until they've checked every angle. They'll have a complete file on me. Now they'll be planning how to handle me."

"You make them sound so conspiratorial, Sam."

"That's what they are. I've got a lot to do before Wednesday morning. What time?"

"Be at the airport at nine-thirty. Mr. Bowman said it will be hot in the Bahamas, and to bring swim clothes and sun clothes. Nothing very formal."

We went through the gate in the garden wall and around to my car in the driveway. "Are you sorry I invited myself aboard?" I asked her.

She looked up at me gravely. She shook her head. "No, Sam. I'm not sorry. I think I feel a little better about everything. I think I snapped at you because I was feeling a little bit guilty. I don't know . . . just what I want to do." She smiled in an apologetic way. "I guess I must be a little mixed up these days."

I swung the car around in front of the garages and headed back down the drive to Walnut Street. I looked in the rear-view mirror and saw her standing in the morning sun in the middle of the wide graveled place, looking small and alone, but standing very straight in her little white shorts and her little red halter, standing with a kind of indelible pride.

As I drove away I felt a bit hot-faced about trying to load her up with the corn-fed speech about the Gurrreat American Way. But, hell, I meant more than half of it. And I had thought there might be a chance she had inherited just a little of her old man's feeling of responsibility not only to the company but to all of Portston.

I had planned to go back to the plant, but decided it could do no harm to advise Tommy McGann of my self-invitation to join the party. That would give me a chance to sound him out about his reaction to Mike Dean. I phoned from a drugstore and their house man said that Mr. and Mrs. McGann were home, and when he came back on the phone he told me to come right out.

Their rangy fieldstone house was in the hills west of town, the only private home in the area with a private airstrip. It was the result of the Texas approach of Tommy's wife, Puss, and at present it accommodated their latest, a sleek and nimble Piper Apache with twin Continentals, retractable tricycle gear. Their house man told me they were out in back. I walked around the house. Tommy was in torn and faded khaki shorts and Puss was in a green swim suit and they were playing some kind of a game with great energy. There was a tall pole set in the lawn with a ball fastened to a long cord tethered to the top of it. They were armed with wooden paddles, and the object seemed to be to whale the ball past your opponent so that the cord wound itself around the pole.

Tommy noticed me first and yelled, "Grab a chair, Sam. Be with you in a couple of minutes, soon as I whup this creature."

I swung one of the chairs by the pool around so that I could watch them. Tommy is thirty-five, eight years older than Louise. They are the same physical type, dark, fine-boned, almost delicate looking. Tommy has Louise's long heavy black lashes, the fine lean hands. But there is nothing at all effeminate about him.

When he was seventeen in 1939, he ran away to Canada and lied his way into the RCAF. He flew an incredible number of missions with the RCAF and the RAF. He bailed out twice, once with burns that kept him three months in the hospital. He transferred over to the American Air Corps in forty-three and flew fifty missions of fighter cover with the Eighth Air Force. Then, over his protests, he was sent back to the states as an instructor. At Randolph Field in Texas, during gunnery practice, a student shot him out of the air. One slug tore away half his jaw. The chute popped open so low that Tommy landed with an impact that gave him, by count, twenty-one fractures when he hit the baked hide of Texas.

Two years later when he hobbled out of the hospital, he was a twenty-four-year-old retired Lieutenant Colonel with an eighty per cent disability pension, with extensive and not entirely successful cosmetic surgery, and with an eighteen-year-old Texas bride called Puss, youngest daughter of an oil and cattle family which gave them, as a wedding present, a few little ole producing wells. He had met her when she had come to the hospital to cheer up the injured.

Tommy refused to spend the rest of his life hobbling about as predicted. Three years later he told the V.A. to cancel the pension. Thomas McGann had tried to get his only son to come into the firm, but Tommy amiably and firmly stated that he had no intention of doing anything constructive. He kept himself busy with his golf, his skin diving, his airplanes and his sports car racing. His only concession to his father was to make Portston his home.

It was very difficult to dislike Tommy and Puss. Their goal seemed to be to be amused, and amusing. At twenty-nine Puss had a sleek and lovely greyhound figure. She had gingery red hair, a cute-ugly face, a nose that was always peeling or ready to peel, a freckled body, a vast capacity for brandy on the rocks, and an attention span as long as a six-year-old's. She had that miraculous physical co-ordination that enabled her to swim, ride, dive, ski, play tennis, golf, badminton, and table tennis with the experts. She had a sprawling, lounging, boyish lack of body consciousness, and no sense of style. Her lipstick and clothes were always the wrong shade. She moved in a welter of broken straps, scuffed shoes, missing buttons, jammed zippers and smudges. She was everyman's tomboy sister—and no woman resented her. You could sense the closeness between Tommy and Puss. It seemed a shame they had no children. They wanted them and would have been good with them.

I sat by the pool and watched them on the green lawn, yelping and panting and beating the bejaysus out of that silly tethered ball. Children at play, lithe and graceful and unselfconscious. In spite of Tommy's frantic lunges, she belted the ball by him and it wound around the post.

He threw the paddle into the air, rumpled her red hair, and they walked toward me, hand in hand, breathing heavily. "Hi, Sam," she said, and went with three running steps toward the pool and in with the oiled perfection of a leaping porpoise.

Tommy dropped into the chair beside mine and shook his head and said, "One day, dammit, I'll find a game I can beat her at. What's on your mind, Sam?"

"I'm going along on the little excursion to the Bahamas."

"Hey, that's wonderful. We'll have a ball. Come on, I want to show you something." I followed him to the garage and up the stairs. With tender loving care he opened a long box, took out a gleaming gizmo, handed it to me and said proudly, "How do you like that?"

I held it and looked at it and said, "I like it fine, but what is it?"

"New spear gun. Just came yesterday. And the

Bahamas is one of the world's best places for skin diving. How's that for timing?"

"That's just fine, too. Tommy, I just came from Louise's house. We had a talk about this Mike Dean and what this might mean to the company."

He took the spear gun from me. "This thing is really built. It's a pilot model, made in West Germany."

"Mike Dean will try to swing you and Louise around to his way of thinking, and everything we've been working for will go to hell."

"There isn't anything on it to corrode. And the balance is perfect. Works on compressed air."

"I'm going along to make sure Mike Dean's team doesn't do a complete snow job on you and Louise."

"Look at the way they've designed this reel attachment, Sam."

"Tommy! Damn it!"

He gave me a quizzical look. "What's the trouble?"

"I think it's a mistake for you and Louise to accept his invitation."

Something seemed to move behind his eyes, something that, for a moment, belied the usual impression of general uselessness. "What's the harm in it, Sam? I don't know why Louise is going. I don't know why you're going. But I'm going for the skin diving. Okay?"

And I couldn't get one inch farther. Back by the pool I refused the offer of a drink and the offer of a swim. I looked back as I left. They were swimming the length of the pool, side by side, in perfect rhythm, and the two fat boxer pups, named Meanie and Moe, were on the pool apron barking their fool heads off.

TWO

WHEN I ARRIVED AT THE PLANT I went directly to Al Dolson's office. Molly, his secretary, said he had gone over to C Building so I asked her to let me know when he got back.

My secretary for the past three years has been Alice Rice, a six-foot, gaunted redhead of forty something years, loyal, efficient, outspoken and pessimistic. I motioned to her as I went through the outer office and she followed me in, book in hand. She sat at the corner of my desk and told me who had called and when and why and jotted down the order in which I wanted her to get them back on the line for me.

"Ready for some overtime, Alice?"

"Oh, Gawd, what now? Just so long as it isn't one of those evening conferences. I despise them."

"By tomorrow night I've got to clean off the whole slate. It shouldn't be too bad. I can dump a lot of stuff on Harry and Andy but I'll have to leave them some poop on progress up to now."

"Even the union thing?"

"That's the only thing we'll shelve until I get back."

"You were going to stay put this week. You had to stay put this week. You said so."

"I know. But I'm going to the Bahamas." She goggled at me. I couldn't resist saying in a whisper, "As a guest of Mike Dean."

It was interesting to watch her changes of expression. Doubt, alarm, suspicion that she was being kidded, and then resignation.

"Don't take it so hard, Alice."

"If I thought you'd sell horses in midstream, Sam Glidden . . ."

I repented and told her why I felt it would be smart to go.

She caught on immediately, and said, "Don't expect to outsmart anybody down there. In that league you're a country boy, too."

"I should take you along."

She ignored that. "How is the prez taking this?" she asked.

"He doesn't know yet. I'll get a call as soon as he gets back to his office. Let's see how many of those phone calls we can get out of the way before he gets back."

I had completed one and was in the middle of the second when Al Dolson came into my office and sat down. Al has the look and bearing of thirty years of commanding combat troops. But he hasn't the assurance to go with it. I hung up and gave it to him between the eyes.

"Mr. and Mrs. Warren Dodge and Mr. and Mrs. Tommy McGann leave Wednesday morning on a private plane to be house guests of Mike Dean in his Bahama hideway, Al."

It took him a full ten seconds to take it in. He licked his lips and his forehead started to sweat. "But . . . Good God, we were all set. Burgeson has their proxies."

"Which won't be worth a damn if they sign new ones."

"They can't do that to us. They've got to be stopped!" His voice was getting shrill.

"Listen, Al. We can't stop them. I've talked to Louise. They're going."

He looked ashen and I saw the signs of his starting to crumble, so I added quickly, "But I'm going along with them. By self-invitation. Dean couldn't refuse because he knows how fishy that would look. I think I can spoil the party."

"Do you really think so?"

"I talked to Louise for over an hour this morning. She's ready to jump either way. Whichever way she jumps, Tommy will jump. I think when the chips are down, she's still on our side."

I didn't feel as confident as I sounded. "How . . . how long will you be gone?" he asked.

"I don't know. Four or five days, I'd guess."

"I thought we'd fought him to a standstill, Sam."

"Nothing has changed yet."

He took a deep breath and let it out. "Tommy doesn't need it, of course; but having no dividends coming in pinches Louise. Tom used to make such a ceremony of giving them the checks himself. Sam, maybe at the June first meeting we could . . . plan to vote say fifty cents a share. You could let her know we plan to do that."

"Al, I think it would be dead wrong to try to buy her. She'd get twenty-five thousand and it would cost us two hundred and twenty thousand we can't spare. If we can't sell our planning on its merits, then it's no damn good. And that two hundred and twenty thousand might be the difference between eventually getting healthy and never quite making it."

He sighed again. "You're right. I know you're right." He looked at me with a savage expression. "That man is a devil, Sam. And he always gets just what he wants."

"Not every time, Al. He misses plenty of times. But his press agents don't mention those times. They want him to be a symbol of infallibility, so the opposition feels licked before the first round starts. I'm not worried yet, Al." I hoped my confident smile didn't look too hollow. I knew that, in one sense, he had more at stake than I did. If Dean plowed up our pea patch, I could find another slot. It wouldn't be easy for Al. It might be impossible. And if Dean wrecked the operation, there wouldn't be anything left in the retirement account.

I managed to prop Al Dolson up again, and realized I was getting tired of that particular ritual.

Alice and I worked until midnight Monday night and until after ten on Tuesday night. I took a longer than usual lunch hour on Tuesday and picked up some "play clothes." I packed a bag Tuesday night and took a cab out to the airport on Wednesday morning. Dean's ship was in when I got there, parked on the apron a hundred yards from the terminal.

It was a C-46. On the rudder assembly was the CAA number and the name Culver Chemical Corporation. I remembered that several years ago Mike Dean had taken over the small corporation and, through stock transfers and mergers, had built it into a big outfit. He was still on the Board of Directors. A slim young man who looked oriental was standing on a wheeled platform loading the luggage into the compartment high on the ship just behind the cockpit. The McGanns and the Dodges stood in the shadow of the wing, chatting with two young men who were evidently the pilot and co-pilot, or, as they like to call themselves, the captain and the pilot.

I went and handed my bag up to the man doing the loading. He smiled his thanks, dogged the hatch, jumped down lightly and started toward the terminal building, pushing the wheeled cart. Louise greeted me warmly and introduced me to our crew. She had a bright look of holiday about her. Tommy Mc-Gann was equally cordial. Puss McGann was elaborately friendly. Warren Dodge gave me a half smile, a remote glance, a slack hand to shake for a half second.

We went aboard. It was outfitted more like a lounge than an airliner. Wall to wall carpeting, wicker armchairs, tables, ash trays, magazines, a little kitchenette and bar. The steward came aboard and the drop door was pulled up and lugged shut.

Moran, the pilot, said, "The weather looks clear and bright all the way, folks. Ricky will fix lunch en

route. We'll make a gas stop at Atlanta, and then stop
at West Palm Beach Airport for clearance. From there
it will be another half hour to West End on Grand
Bahama Island. You'll go the rest of the way by boat.
We should put you down on Grand Bahama at four
o'clock, and that means you should be at Dubloon Cay
in time for the cocktail hour. In the meanwhile, if
you'd like an eye-opener to start the day, Ricky will
be glad to fix you up."

Warren Dodge waited until we were airborne before demanding a whisky sour, easy on the sugar,
boy. Tom and Puss both thought that sounded fine.
Louise said she'd wait a while. I asked if there was
cold beer. There was; and it was imported and
delicious.

I was the guest who had invited himself, and I did
not feel at ease. Perhaps, with that quartet, I wouldn't
have felt at ease under the very best of circum-
stances. I'd come from mill people. Three generations
of Gliddens had worked at the Harrison Corporation.
I had, in the last seven years, acquired a certain
amount of ease and polish, but it was acquired. These
people had grown up with the certain knowledge that
if they wanted anything badly enough, it would be
given to them. Spiritually, I was closer to Mike Dean.
If I wanted anything, I had to go get it.

But the stratification wasn't that simple. It could
not be called the case of the noble working man
versus the idle and decadent rich. Certainly damn
little nobility in the working man at Harrison in the
past few years. Not the way work standards were set.
I am no bloated capitalistic exploiter, but some of
the situations in our shop sickened me. The way
standards were set, on some operations, a man could
perform in two hours what we had to pay for on the
basis of an eight-hour day. They were running bridge
tournaments in the employee lounges. They saw all
the afternoon ball games on television. And they were
getting a wise-guy boot out of using union strength

to screw management. It was a cynicism and a "me first" approach to life which was in its way just as empty and destructive as Tommy and Warren's complete idleness. The low productivity per employee was crippling us. A new union contract was coming up in November. I knew they were going to yelp for more money. I was going to go along with the demand for more money provided the union would play fair on work standards.

"Deep black thoughts?" Louise asked over the sound of the airplane.

"World on my shoulders," I said, grinning at her.

Warren Dodge had taken the chair on the other side of me just in time to hear the last remark. "You like to give the impression of being all burdened down with big deals, don't you, Glidden?"

I turned and looked at the puffy, sullen and arrogant face. Warren Dodge is a big man. I think he is two years older than I am, but I like to believe he looks ten years older. His blond hair is thin. Liquor has puffed the big body, ravaged the school-boy face. But there is still a curiously collegiate flavor about him, the forlorn echoes of a valiant goal-line stand in the mud of a November afternoon. His people had been enormously wealthy, and had been almost completely wiped out in 1934 when Warren was about nine years old. There was one little trust fund that the creditors couldn't get at. It put Warren through Choate and Princeton, and then there was nothing left. For a few years between preparatory school and Princeton, I believe, he was an enlisted marine, and received a medical discharge. After Princeton he played amateur tennis that was so close to being top flight he was able to live off it.

Louise met him when she was twenty-four at a house party when she went to visit, in Philadelphia, the girl who had been her roommate at Wellesley. Tom McGann, her father, was violently opposed to her marrying a tennis bum. He'd given up hope of

Tommy ever coming into the firm, and he had hoped she would marry somebody whom he could take in. But she was twenty-four and she had an income, mostly from Harrison dividends, of about a hundred and fifty thousand dollars a year. It had made a nice soft berth for Warren because his drinking had begun to soften his tennis game. And he was nearly thirty. She had married him the second week she knew him, and they had been in Italy three months on their honeymoon when Tom's death called them back. And it had turned out not to be such a soft berth for Warren. She couldn't support him in the way he expected to be supported.

Warren Dodge was spoiling for a quarrel. Even though alcohol had softened him up, I wasn't anxious to go around and around with him. He'd had some police trouble in Portston. He was known as a fast, vicious and merciless brawler.

"A big deal every day, Warren," I said.

He took a gulp of his drink. "Tell Mike Dean about all your big deals. Don't try to tell me. Maybe Mike will tell you what a big deal is."

"Don't be tiresome, dear," Louise said.

"Tiresome! Ho, ho! Glidden is the tiresome one, honey. He's been taking you in with all this crap about backing up the dear old family corporation. So you say: okay, no dividends. So they give each other unlimited expense accounts and pay raises and God knows what all. I'm sick of your being a sucker, honey."

"Knock it off, knock it off!" Tommy McGann said, standing and swaying with the slight movement of the plane, grinning down at Warren out of his broken face. "What the hell do you know about big finance? I wouldn't let you make change of a dollar, you Princeton phony."

All the marks of anger went out of Warren's face and he beamed up at Tommy. "Just a crazy flyboy," he said. I have never been able to understand why the two brothers-in-law get along so well. It could be their mutual idleness, but that does not have the same flavor. Tommy makes a brisk business of doing nothing. And there is something sour and destructive about Warren Dodge's inertia.

Tommy had said only a few words to Warren, but they had taken the edge of his belligerence away.

"Be good," Tommy said. "Be good to our Sam Glidden. He is a member of the family. I shall now go forward and trade lies with my fellow intrepid birdmen and beg a chance to hand-fly this raunchy old craft."

After Tommy had gone forward, Warren turned back toward me, and I could guess from his expression that he was going to be sincere and earnest.

"It's like this, Sam. I figure this is our chance for Harrison to go big time. If we get under Mike Dean's wing, it's going to help us a lot. If we go big time, we could have an executive airplane like this one."

"And that would be handy, I suppose."

"Certainly. Louise and I have a big enough block of stock so I don't understand, Sam, why I haven't been put on the Board. I don't see why Walt Burgeson should be voting our stock."

His childish picture of himself was all too vivid. Warren Dodge, member of the Board of Directors of the Harrison Corporation, flew to Chicago yesterday to attend an industry conference.

But it was a little too late for Warren Dodge.

It was too late for him by the time he got out of Princeton, because by then he had learned what he could procure with nothing but a boyish grin and the bulge of tennis muscles.

"It might be a good idea for you to be on the Board, Warren," I said. "Al Dolson and I are responsible to the Board, and so are the other corporate officers. We like to have people on the Board who understand the special problems we're facing. When we get back I'd be glad to arrange it so that you can come in and work in the various divisions of the company and get the whole picture."

He gave me an uneasy glance. "What kind of work?"

"Start you off as a stock chaser. That's the fastest way to learn. In about eighteen months you'd have a pretty good background."

He nodded dubiously and said something about getting another leg to stand on, and went back to Ricky's department with his empty glass.

"That wasn't very kind, Sam," Louise said.

"I mean it seriously. If he'll come in, I think it would be good for him."

"It must be nice to sit way up there and look down upon all of us and decide what's good for us."

I felt my face get hot. "I didn't mean it to sound that way. I just meant that . . ."

"You meant that he does nothing and that makes you uneasy because everybody should be brisk and industrious like you."

"Damn it, Louise, you don't . . ."

She smiled in a tired way. "Sorry. Pay absolutely no attention." She hitched her chair toward the window and began to look down at the green and misted earth below, and I knew I had been dismissed.

Puss was across the way playing solitaire at a small table. After one venture into the whisky sour area, she was back to her normal brandy on the rocks. I went over and sat opposite her and said, "Black ten on the red jack."

"Oh, I know all about that, Sam. I'm saving it for when there isn't anything else left to do. How about some gin?" Tommy was up front between the pilots, bending over them and talking. Warren had sat down in the rear of the plane and was looking at a magazine. Louise was looking out the window, and her look of holiday had faded.

"For how much?" I asked Puss.

She bit her lip. "Hmmm. How interesting do we want to make it? Dime a point?"

"That's too damn interesting. That would make my hands sweat. A nickel?"

"Done. Cut for deal."

By the time Ricky served lunch, I was a hundred and eighty-eight dollars to the good and she was furious at me, at the cards and at herself. She is a girl with a highly developed competitive instinct. By the time we made the gas stop she had gotten forty dollars back and she was bored with the game. She scrawled a check on her Texas bank.

We made West Palm on schedule, landing amid the heavy civilian and Air Force traffic on the joint base, and it took fifteen minutes to get clearance to West End.

Warren had drunk himself into a semi-catatonic state, sleepily and massively out of touch with reality. The rest of us looked out the windows as we flew east over Palm Beach, over the big hotels and the random blue patchwork of swimming pools, out over the Atlantic surf line. In twenty-five minutes we began to see the islands of the Bahamas, the vividly streaked blue and tan and green of the shoal waters of the Bahama Flats.

I saw a huge waterfront establishment which, except for an enormous swimming pool, looked from the air like some sort of military base. A narrow paved road ran along the shoreline to a ramshackle village about a mile away, and continued on through the village and down the coast. Except for the big establishment and the village, the rest of what I could see of the narrow island looked overgrown and uninhabited.

We landed on a paved, eroded airstrip and taxied to the terminal building. It was a small frame building surrounded with dust. It had a stubby tower, and had at one time been painted gaily but the colors had faded. Across the taxi strip from the terminal several light planes were parked and lashed.

As we went down the steps a man came toward the

aircraft, walking briskly and smiling warmly. He seemed impervious to the grubby surroundings of the airport. At forty feet he radiated impressive charm and complete efficiency. He wore sand-colored walking shorts, a chocolate-brown sports shirt, a yachting cap, Allan Murray Space Shoes in a sandal design with tall dark-brown wool socks. His exposed knees were sturdy and dark brown, the hair on them bleached pale. He was tall, with solid shoulders and a handsome rather heavy face. He had a wide white smile and he was theatrically gray at the temples. As a television huckster he would have been termed true and valid. I had the uncomfortable feeling that you could be marooned on an island with this fellow for seven years and never get a clue as to what he was thinking. He would be inevitably and interminably polite and charming, and were he forced to kill you and eat you, he would be deft and slightly apologetic and quite noble about it. And he would know exactly which leaves and berries to boil with you to give you the right flavor.

He went directly to Louise and took her hand in both of his and made like Gregory Peck being a young girl's uncle and said, "I'm so glad you could make it, Louise. Mike sends his apologies. There're other guests on the island and he couldn't get away or he would have met you himself. Hello, Tommy." The handshake was both manly and Ivy League.

Louise introduced him to Puss, and then to Warren. Warren had a ponderous list and a bleared expression. And she said, "And Sam Glidden, Fletcher Bowman."

I got the manly handshake. He looked directly into my eyes, unwaveringly. It is an unnatural affectation and it always makes me feel uneasy. "Glad you could join the party, Sam. Mike is delighted. He's been following your career, and we both feel you can make valid contributions to our little conference on the island."

"Uh. Thanks," I said. I wished I could have been glib. I wished he'd let go of my hand. He made me feel as if I were wearing coveralls and chewing a kitchen match.

"I'll get your stuff hustled through customs," he said. "And I've lined up three so-called taxis. Don't be alarmed by them. They'll get us to the Grand Bahama Club. It's only three quarters of a mile away. Our boat is tied up at the club dock and we'll have a fifty-minute run to Dubloon Cay. Suppose you all wait over there in the shade and we'll hustle the baggage off."

When we were in the shade of the terminal building I looked back. He was talking to the crew and they were bobbing their heads. Two Bahama boys were helping Ricky get the luggage off. I had the same big old brown scuffed suitcase I had taken to college. There was a big case that I imagined belonged to Tommy. Both women seemed to have four matched pieces each.

All the baggage went in one cab, and Fletcher Bowman split us, three and three, in the other two cabs. He managed to arrange it so he rode with Louise and me. I felt quite certain that he knew that we were the two to focus on.

We got a brisk travelogue. "The airstrip belongs to the Grand Bahama Club. Chap named Butlin built the Grand Bahama Club after the war. A British syndicate operation. Put millions into it. But nobody had figured out how to get the people here to fill it. It went broke and sat empty until a few years ago and then another group took it over. They seem to be doing well enough. They put the income back into improvements. It's really quite comfortable. See those buildings there. Completely empty. Moldering away. I doubt the hotel will ever get large enough to put them to use. But the plantings are nice, aren't they? Here we are. This is the part they use now."

The part in use was huge. We went on into the

lobby. It was airy and vast and pleasantly decorated. We could look out through glass walls at wide green lawns, brilliant flowers, stone walks, several acres of awning in wide blue and white stripes, the gigantic swimming pool, and the vivid waters of the Bahama Flats beyond the coconut palms.

I saw Warren take his bearings, turn and head directly for the bar off the lobby.

"If you like," Bowman said, "you people can have a quick drink or take a quick look around. I'll see to the luggage and meet you down there on the dock in ten minutes. That's our boat, tied up on the left side, the green and white one." He smiled and nodded and marched off.

Tommy and Puss headed for the bar. "Look around?" I asked Louise. She was looking hesitantly toward the bar.

She gave me a bright and completely artificial smile and said, "Let's."

We walked out a door and by a large airy dining room with yellow tablecloths and headed for the swimming pool.

"Your Mister Bowman is quite a production. Has Dean got many more at home like him?"

"He's not my Mister Bowman and I wouldn't know."

"Don't snap at me, Louise."

"I'm sorry. I guess I just feel . . . sort of cross. Anyway, I think he's very nice."

"Do you know anything about him?"

"He said he'd been with Mike Dean for quite a long time."

"He's a very plausible guy."

"Sam, will you look at that poor little mouse on the high board? She waited too long."

There was an awkward girl in that gangly hinterland between childhood and adolescence on the high board. She wore a brown swim suit. She stood pigeon-toed, holding her nose, her left hand outstretched for balance. She was looking down at the water and she was frozen there. Her friends were yelling at her to jump. After a painful eternity, she turned and scampered back to the safety of the platform. A small boy jeered at her and ran out on the board and off the end and made running movements all the way down. The girl clung to the iron railing, shaking her head. I looked at Louise. She was looking up at the girl, her lips slightly parted, an odd expression on her face.

"That's me," she said softly.

"What?"

She turned quickly and the mood was lost. "I . . . I don't know what I meant. I didn't mean anything." So the muted and competent Louise Dodge felt somehow that she was on a high place and afraid to jump. Maybe she felt she had waited too long. And I wondered if, also, she felt she were in some area of transition, some awkward area between two kinds of existences.

We walked to the far end of the big pool.

"Look," I said.

The girl had gone out to the end of the board again. Her friends were counting aloud, chanting a count. Shrill voices saying, "Three, four, five, six, seven, eight, nine, ten—GO!"

She wavered and could not. She started to turn and lost her balance. She waved her arms wildly and screamed and fell, and grabbed her nose when she was half way down. We watched her swim to the side, race up the ladders, run out to the end of the board and go off almost without hesitation.

"After the first time, it's easy," I said.

"That's what they say," Louise said.

Somehow we had started talking on two levels. It made me feel clumsy with her, and yet curiously excited. I could not deny the strength of the attraction I felt toward her. I could not look at her without thinking how it would be to touch her. But it was something I was going to have to sublimate. I knew

that. And this funny sort of talk made it more difficult
to thrust desire out of my mind. I did not want to
think of desire, because then I thought of Warren
Dodge, and my mind would make ugly, sick little
pictures of the two of them together, of his grossness
defiling her lucently ivory body. Somebody had
written the wrong story book about Louise and Sam.
We didn't meet when we should have met. When we
were both ready to meet. A time like that goes by and
you can't get it back. You can howl or you can whine,
but you can't go back to any of those forks in your
own road and try the other turn instead of the one you
took.

Anyway, this wasn't the girl with the braid and the
blue dress. This was a woman and she was twenty-
seven, and you could look at her eyes and the shape
of her mouth and make a fair guess as to how often
and how badly she had been hurt.

When we saw the others down on the dock we
headed that way. The boat was called the *Try Again*,
and it was a twenty-six-foot sports fisherman with out-
riggers, twin screws, two swivel fishing chairs bolted
to the deck, a broad beam and an oversized cockpit.
The crew was a knotted charcoal-colored little man
in khakis named Romeo. When we were aboard, some
boys on the dock tossed our lines aboard. Romeo
eased it out and then opened it up and it really got up
and went. There was a northeast wind and enough of
a chop so that the *Try Again* spanked white spray
out fifteen yards on each side of the bow, but it ran
steady and dry.

Bowman, braced easily against the movement of
the boat, gave us all more of the travelogue, speaking
above the sound of the gutty engines.

"This is one of the great fishing areas of the world,"
he said. "You have the flats for dolphin, albacore,
king, tarpon, barracuda, amberjack, Spanish mackerel
and so on. Then, down toward Bimini, which isn't

much of a run from here in the *Try Again*, you get
marlin, tuna, sail, mako, the big stuff. Mike doesn't
get as much time to fish as he'd like to have. He's a
real bug on it. The day before yesterday he got an
eighty-seven-pound barracuda on thirty-pound test
line. Ugly devil.'"

I couldn't resist it. "I thought you were in New
York the day before yesterday, Mr. Bowman."

It didn't cause a ripple. "Please call me Fletcher,
Sam. I got down yesterday. Amparo showed me a
picture of it she took with one of those Polaroid
cameras. That's Amparo Blakely. She's Mike's indispensable girl Friday. Last year Mike brought a four-
hundred-and-thirty-pound marlin to gaff on sixty-
pound test line. The fight lasted over three hours."

Tommy had been listening avidly. He moved in
on Bowman with what sounded like highly technical
questions. Bowman seemed to give informed answers.
It gave me the uneasy feeling that there would be
damn few subjects that could come up that Bowman
wouldn't have the inside pitch on, and couldn't dis-
cuss with mellow confidence and self-effacing charm.
He had a white scar in one thick black eyebrow
and I wondered who had had the pleasure of putting
it there. The sun was hot and the three male tourists,
Tommy first, shed jackets and ties and rolled up shirt
sleeves. The air seemed to be reviving Warren. He
asked Bowman if there was a drink aboard. Bowman
was apologetic and dreadfully sorry that there was
not. But we would be at Dubloon Cay in half an hour
now. It was just thirty miles northeast of Grand
Bahama.

I found myself looking at Louise. She was standing
by the rail, holding onto one vertical support for the
Navy top. The wind snapped her glossy black hair
against her cheek and molded her dress tightly against
her high breasts and against her thighs. I just looked
at her and when I turned and looked at Bowman he

was still talking to Tommy, but he was looking over Tommy's shoulder at me. He held my glance for a quarter beat and then looked away, but I had the feeling he had gotten the message.

THREE

BOWMAN POINTED OUT DUBLOON CAY and it didn't look as though there was anything on it. It was low and about three miles long. Then we went around a point and we could see the small tidy bay, the long T-shaped dock, a wide expanse of lawn that sloped up to a long low building of weathered wood, with many porches and verandas. As we came closer I could see a pool to the left of the house, with umbrellas and people lying around in the sun, and a tiny figure of somebody in a white coat carrying a tray of drinks. To the right of the main house, back in the pines, were several smaller structures. There was a cruiser about forty-five feet long moored to the dock, as well as several skiffs with outboard motors. A hundred yards to the left of the dock, along the semicircle of sand beach, a small float plane was pulled up against the sand and moored with long lines tied to palms. There was a low sea wall between the lawn and the sand beach. The layout looked like a small and efficient hotel, fashionable and comfortable. God knows Mike Dean could afford it.

Romeo reversed the engines at the last possible moment and Bowman fended the boat off the dock until Romeo had the fenders in place and the lines secured. Two Bahamian boys in white jackets trotted down and got the luggage onto the dock. We each identified our own luggage, and Bowman told the boys what rooms we were to be put in, and told us that the best thing to do would be follow the boys and unpack and change into something comfortable and join the party out by the pool. He said it was a

39

little too late for sun clothing as the bugs would be out in another hour to drive us all indoors.

We were all in the right wing of the building. The McGanns were beside me and the Dodges beyond them. My room was clean and rather bare and very small. A room for sleeping only. There was a small tiled bath. One door opened onto the corridor and the other door onto the long front veranda with its view of the bay and the open sea beyond, and twin islands in the distance. I unpacked, changed to gray slacks and a dark blue sports shirt, and walked out onto the veranda at about five-thirty. The sun was getting lower, but there was still a lot of heat in it. I had no intention of heading for the pool by myself.

Fifty feet along the screened veranda a screen door hissed. I looked up from lighting my cigarette and saw a blond girl come in, walking from sunlight into shade. She wore a knit shirt in a narrow red and white stripe, red shorts that were very short indeed. She was a round-faced leggedy blonde, toffee-tan, barefoot, humming a something song, swinging her legs in the song's rhythm, carrying a half drink in her hand. She saw me and lifted the drink as though in a toast and said, "Hello now," and turned into a room two doors from mine. She left me with memories of legs and smile, and a sense of the whole island being brought into better focus. I sat in a deep canvas chair and put my legs on a low round wooden table, and in a few minutes Tommy and Puss came out. We decided to wait for the others and it was not a long wait, and then we went on out to the pool where everybody was, and where the drinks were.

I had seen plenty of pictures of Michael Davis Dean, and I had heard a lot of talk about him. I knew what he would look like. A big head with heavy features of that spuriously noble design that makes you think of togas and Cicero. A shock of prematurely white hair, unkempt in the contrived way of a second-

rate poet. Nobody seemed to know very much about
his past. His father had been well off. Mike had never
gone to college. He got his first national publicity
back in 1934 when he was thirty. In the big receiver-
ship tangle over the Geiss Roller Bearing empire, it
was Mike who popped up out of no place, holding
aces back to back. He had never married. I had heard
a lot of words about him. Crafty, unscrupulous,
power-mad, egomaniac. And also, charming, able,
generous, genius.

I was not braced for Mike in the flesh. He had a
deep tan and he wore a straw coolie hat and an ankle-
length pink sarong, professionally knotted at the waist
and thoroughly rump-sprung. He was shorter than
he had looked in his pictures; he stood about five-
nine. There were hard shifting slabs of muscle in his
back and shoulders and chest, and the sarong was
knotted around a slightly protruding belly that looked
hard as a rock. His eyes were a very pale gray-blue,
and his chest hair was heavy and white. He had
something of a Hawaiian look about him. He radiated
intense energy, and a conspicuous charm. It was almost impossible to imagine him in any group he
would not dominate merely on the basis of an animal
magnetism. I sensed that this was a man who would
commit himself one hundred and ten percent to anything he decided to do. I sensed that it would be a
sorry situation to be standing in his way.

Fletcher Bowman introduced us. Mike was, be-
wilderingly, a jolly and muscular elder brother to
Puss, a courtly uncle to Louise, a drinking partner
to Warren Dodge, a fellow sportsman to Tommy, all
in the space of a minute and a half. When he released my hand he grinned shrewdly up at me
and thumped me lightly in the ribs with a slow fist
big as a burl of mahogany, and said in a voice the
others could not hear, "We'll make some talk when
we get a chance, Big Sam."

And the hell of it was that it made me feel flattered and honored to be given this special attention, even though I knew it was only a part of his tactics. "I'm the uninvited guest," I said.

"Self-invited. And the only reason for that is because I didn't think there was a chance you'd come. You fit right into this picture the way we want to set it up, Sam. Folks, you'll need a drink before we make the rounds. No, Fletcher, I'll take them around."

He motioned and one of the white-coated men came over and took our drink order. Mike was drinking steaming coffee from a pewter mug with a glass bottom. A small boy with a white jacket and great dignity came over to us and offered a tray of hors d'oeuvres.

Mike rapped him on the top of the crinkly skull and the boy grinned with quick pleasure and worship. "This is Skylark," he said. "Romeo and Ruby's youngest. Romeo and Ruby stay here on the island the year round and keep things in shape. When I move in with a crowd, they beef up the staff with their relatives and stock up on food and liquor."

Our drinks came and Mike took us on a circuit of the pool. I knew it would take quite a little while before I could fit names to the faces. But there was one that was easy. Bonny Carson. I had expected to find at least one person from the entertainment world there, but I would not have guessed it would be Bonny. She hit her peak in the late forties and early fifties when she starred in several hit musicals. Outside of infrequent guest spots on television, she had dropped out of sight. But the big-eyed clown face was unmistakable. She had strong gifts of comedy, and a brass voice with which she could lift the roof off the house when she belted out a song. But on a Wednesday evening, the tenth of May, on Dubloon Cay, she was solemnly and somewhat sullenly drunk, and she was showing her thirty-five-plus years. There was a little man hovering around her, name of Bundy. He had a sharp pale nervous face, more than his

quota of nervous mannerisms: ear tugging, head
scratching, lip pulling. His smile went off and on like
a timed electric sign. In shorts he looked somewhat
like the pictures you have seen of self-conscious
chickens defeathered by a tornado. He had a fiercely
protective attitude toward Bonny Carson.

There was another woman who stood out, Amparo Blakely, Mike Dean's indispensable secretary.
She would have been noticed anywhere. She was big.
She was nearly six feet tall, and she was big-boned
and she was close to forty; but none of those attributes
detracted from her look of being a completely feminine
and forceful and desirable woman. I had seen her in
photographs featuring Mike Dean. In those pictures
she had usually been a few steps behind him. I had
not realized how big she was, but I had a clear memory
of her striking face. I knew that Amparo was a not
unusual Spanish name and I had wondered if she was
partly Spanish. But now, seeing her in the flesh, I
suspected that she was half Mexican Indian. Though
her eyes were pale, her face, tanned to a red-bronze,
had that Aztecan look of humid passions hidden behind the Indio mask.

I had heard the many legends of Mike Dean's Amparo Blakely. It was said that she had become in-
dependently wealthy by riding along with Mike on
his deals. She had been with him a long time. And
now, with ease and assurance, she was acting as his
hostess. I had heard it hinted that their relationship
was more than professional. As I looked at her, at
the mature, magnificent and superb body in a white
and aqua dress, I did not see how any platonic relationship between Mike and this total woman would
be possible. They both had a look of being more alive
than the rest of us.

Her hair was dark when she was in the shade, but
the sun brought out coppery glints in it. She wore
crude gold earrings in a barbaric design. And as she
moved among the guests she had that inimitable look

of being utterly at home in her world and within herself.

I looked around and I knew there were one hell of a lot more people on the island than I had expected, and I knew I should get them all sorted out as quickly as possible. I wanted to know who was working for and with Mike Dean, directly and indirectly. You can tell a lot about a man by the attitude of the people who work for him. Fletcher Bowman was a younger, more suave, less forceful edition of Mike Dean. But he was so obscured behind all his masks of mannerisms I could not detect his actual attitude toward his boss man.

I wanted information and so I looked around and detected what I thought might be the most pleasant way of acquiring it. The blond cutie I had seen on the veranda was back at the pool, and she had changed to a blue blouse and a white skirt. She sat on a couch built like a trampoline, a yellow canvas cover spring-fastened to a tubular bronze frame. She had a new drink and she was humming her little song and half-smiling into the middle distance and tapping a slender foot in a tall blue shoe as she sat facing a dull fireball of a sun that was sliding down into a sea that had turned to oiled slate.

I stood over her and said, "On the first go-round I got it that you're called Murphy, but I didn't get the rest of it. And I'm lousy on names and so I need maybe a briefing on you and the rest of the throng."

She came back out of her middle distance and focused on me, warm and friendly as a pup.

"In my file folder it says here that you're the biggest thing on the island and your name is Sam Something."

"Glidden."

"Have it your way. And I am a shade drunk from drinking, and you may sit down and be briefed." She patted the yellow canvas beside her and I sat down. "About this Murphy," she said, "I am Bridget Hallowell and I used to be called Bridey until that damn book came out and then it became Murphy. I am starting an international movement to get it back to Bridget where it belongs."

"Bridget it will be. And on the briefing, start with you."

"After I get you lined away. First I want the measurements. Men shouldn't be so big. I do not mind being made to feel dainty and fragile, but not *this* dainty and fragile."

It is something I have had to get used to. "Six feet four and a quarter, Bridget. Two hundred and eighteen pounds. And I will be thirty-one on the twenty-fourth of next July. I am vice-president of the Harrison Corporation."

"And unmarried."

"How do you know that?"

"Well, it shows a little. Sort of. Anyway, dear Fletcher told me you were when he told me to be nice to you on account of you are not matched up with any female and social situations seem to go better by twos, so I am your girl, sort of. So you better chide me for being a little drunk, and maybe give me a hurt look. You know you look more like thirty-five."

"Gosh, thanks."

"I expect it's from being so big. Now about me, I am now leading this here mad gay life I dreamed about. It is like this. Long, long ago when I was a mere child of sorts, I won a short story contest and so, natch, I wrote a novel. But it was stinky. And then I sold some nauseating gloop to the love magazines, and then I packed up, I did, and I went to New York, I did, and freelancing was too too rough so I went on a magazine and I wrote how-to things. How to keep mealy bugs out of your screened terrace. What to do about adolescent acne. And then I got married and I should have researched something called how to stay married because it was going terribly sour after only five months and then he resolved it on the

Sawmill River Parkway by slewing off it into a big maple tree; and that was November last year, and now I am a fledgling with Brainerd Associates, which is a small and very rich and very discreet public relations firm. Over there, talking to Fletcher Bowman, you will see a terribly sincere man named Guy Brainerd. The one with the bald head and all the chin. He is my boss man. Mike Dean pays the firm a fabulous sum every year to make Mike Dean a wholesome household word, and I have been assigned to the Dean account, and so I was brang down on the airplane like one of the brass." She turned and gave me an odd look and said, "Don't get things mixed up, Samuel. I am pretty damn good at what I am doing."

"I'm sure you are."

"This empty-looking head is not that empty. I don't know why you make me feel I should explain myself. Anyhow, look over there at the end of the pool, at the gal with the sleek blond hairdo and the sleek blond manners and all the jangle bracelets and the poison green shorts tailored to that saucy little rump. That is Elda Garry and she is a lady editor on *Blend*, and we have her almost talked into running a great big warm feature on Mike Dean, his philosophies and philanthropies. Elda and my boss are having a thing, and it has been going on for some little time now, and it is very handy for them to come down here, and I suspect I was brought along to make it look a little better, maybe. Guy's wife is pure undiluted bitch, and isn't it funny that in getting away from her, he'll run right to more of the same? Golly, I bet you didn't know you'd get briefed this good."

"It's thorough," I said.

"Let us continue. The guy Elda is talking to is Cam Duncan. He's a lawyer and he works for Mike." I had noticed Duncan when we were introduced. He was in his thirties, a tall, shambling, frail-looking man with mouse-colored hair and an engagingly ugly face and a crooked and charming grin. "He's a honey bug," said Bridget.

"How about the ageing ranch hand?" I asked. "The one talking to Mrs. McGann." He was a faded man in weary khakis and a big pale sombrero, with a cud in his cheek. I hadn't quite caught his name when we were taken around, but Puss had caught it and given a little squeal of delight and the man had told her he hadn't seen her, by God, since she was so little she had to climb the corral fence to get on a horse.

"Puhleeze!" Bridget said. "You are referring to Porter Crown of Crown Ranch, Tex-Crown Oil, Crown-Arabian Oil, Crown-Dean Aviation Devices, et cetera."

"I beg your pardon."

"Personally I think he is an old floopph. The harem job on his left is his third wife, Tessy. She's got an accent a hatchet would bounce off. Hungarian, I think." Mrs. Crown, in Italian beach wear, was an abundant redhead who seemed to be constantly in a half doze, pearly and sexual. "That fifty-foot hunk of brass and mahogany at the dock, the *Portess*, is theirs. Port calls it their 'little boat.' He keeps it and the big boat at Padre Island. There's a crew of two who sleep aboard. The big chunk of muscles who just started talking to Bonny Carson is named Jack Buck. He has the strong impression he's irresistible. He crews the *Portess*. Port is democratic, so Jack Buck gets to eat and swim and drink with the folks. But the democracy does not extend to Fidelio. He's the little Mexican chef and steward on the boat. They brought the *Portess* across the Gulf and around the Keys and up here to the Bahamas. Port and Tessy and Port's daughter."

"Which one is she?"

"You'll meet her later. She's about nineteen and she looks like a gypsy and I hear tell she's just about as wild as one. This little cruise is to get her mind off somebody old Port didn't approve of. She's the only child of his second marriage. I think she's a brat. Her name is Lolly, from Laura, and old Port calls her

Lollypop. She drank hard and folded early. Now where am I?"

"Who is the Bundy character with Bonny Carson?"

"Some kind of a manager. He's trying to swing something with Mike. God only knows what. Turn-about is fair play, Sam'l. All I know about your group is that some of them are named McGann and some are named Dodge, and they have big chunks of stock in this Harrison thing Mike is interested in. Who belongs to whom?"

"The dark girl is Louise Dodge, and the beefy one over there is Warren Dodge."

"She doesn't look very happy. So the other two are McGanns. The male McGann is kinda cute."

"He's Louise Dodge's brother."

One of the white-coated Bahamians came to us for a drink order. "More of the same, please, John," she said, and put her empty glass on his tray. I asked for another, also. When he went away I said, "How big a staff is there?"

"Seven, if you count that adorable little Skylark."

"Are there any missing guests, besides Lolly Crown?"

She made a count of the group. "Nope. Seventeen counting everybody. Then, with Fidelio, there are twenty-five on Dubloon Cay. What they call a mixed group. Maybe a mixed-up group." She turned on the poolside cot and tucked her knees under her and looked directly at me and said, "Are you here to try to knock a couple of spokes out of Mike's big wheel?"

"What gives you that idea, Bridget?"

"I heard them wondering about you on the airplane, Fletcher Bowman and Cam Duncan. I was supposed to be asleep but I wasn't, quite."

"They say anything I should know?" I asked easily.

"I just got the idea they think you're pretty bright and it may take some selling to sell you on whatever they have in mind."

"They don't have to sell me. They just have to sell

the Dodges and the McGanns. I don't own any stock
in Harrison. I work for wages. I work for the owners."

The question she had put to me bothered me. One
moment everything had seemed very casual, and
then her question had made it look like a stage setting
again. As though Mike Dean's organization had
planted all these people by the pool and cued them
very carefully. It was like being with a small group
of friends at a very big and very busy roulette table,
and suddenly having a strong hunch that every other
gambler at the table was a shill for the house.

A lazy black mosquito landed on her arm, ready to
feed. She slapped it and said, "The nightly visitors
are beginning to move in. Look at that sun, Sam!
Half gone, and not a cloud. It looks like a red-hot
rivet in a steel plate. Let's take our drinks and I'll
give you a short tour of inspection, like the one Elda
Garry and I were given. Guy Brainerd has been here
before."

She showed me the house, the main lounge, the
game room, the gleaming kitchen with its hotel equipment and the servants fixing dinner. She knew them by
name and introduced them and they seemed to like
her. It was hard to believe she had been down only a
little longer than one full day. Ruby, Romeo's wife,
was a massive woman. The only other female servant
was named Booty. She seemed to be about eighteen or
nineteen. She was Ruby's niece. She was quite tall,
and luxuriantly, splendidly constructed. She was the
color of cocoa, and the skin of her face had an un-
believably fine texture. Her mouth was heavy and
Negroid, her nose fine and slim, her eyes like the eyes
in the ancient drawings of Egyptian women. She
masked shyness with a dignified reserve; and when she
walked she bent forward slightly from the waist and
did not swing her arms, as though to hide from the
world the new ripeness of breasts and belly.

When we left the kitchen, Bridget told me that
Booty was glad to have this extra work because she

was soon to be married to a man who captained one of the charter boats that operated out of the Grand Bahama Club.

We started down a path in the rear of the building, but the bugs were out in too much force. We hurried back and Bridget said, "Nothing too spectacular down there anyway. Just a big generator house and the well house and the pumps and a big storage tank. Over there is where the servants live."

"Who owns the little float plane?"

"Golly, I forgot all about them! Change the count to nineteen and twenty-seven total. It belongs to a man named Bert Buford. Mike is in on some big land syndicate deal in Broward County north of Miami, and Bert is the resident manager of one of the developments they've started. Bert flies over quite often with his wife, whether or not Mike is here. He comes for the fishing. The wife is named Margaret Mary. And you have to say the whole name. She's a southrun type girl. They've been out in one of the skiffs and they should be back by now. And, by golly, there they come."

They had come from the east and turned into the bay. The outboard made a rackety sound in the fading day. We went down onto the dock, and Romeo came down to help and before the skiff had come up to the dock, Guy Brainerd and Elda Garry, and Tommy and Louise had joined us. Louise gave me a quick look of question and I knew she was wondering about this sudden friendship with the girl they called Murphy.

Guy Brainerd said, "The others are too blasé to walk down to look at a fish. Just us greenhorns."

"I gave up fishing when I was terribly young," Elda Garry said in her mid-Manhattan accent. "A boy expected me to put a perfectly horrible looking thing on my own hook. I think it was called a damnittohell or something like that."

"Hellgrammite," Bridget said tersely. "Aquatic larva of the dobson."

"*Really*, darling, that little head of yours is positively *stuffed* with things. It should have been called a damnittohell, because when I tried, it bit me, and I haven't been fishing since. My God, look at the size of that thing!"

The man in the skiff had stood up and eased a big fish onto the dock. It was streaked with gorgeous shades of blue and green and gold. The man was knobbly and towheaded and he had the pinched untannable face of the cracker. He wore a baseball cap, a T-shirt and jeans sawed off at the knees. "There's a right good albacore, Romeo," he said. "Hi, folks. Hi, Murph. I'm Bert Buford and this here's my wife, Margaret Mary." She was dark and comfortable looking and she made me remember an object I hadn't thought of in years. It had belonged to my mother. It was a plump little pincushion in the shape of a kitten.

Bridget took care of the introductions and Tommy helped Margaret Mary up onto the dock, and we watched the other fish off-loaded as Bert identified them. "Little amberjack. Couple of yallatails. Nice red snapper. But the 'cuda about to drive us nuts out there today."

"What are those outfits?" Tommy asked.

"These here are a couple of Rumer Atlantic surf-casting spinners," Buford said. "I got 'em on hollow glass spinning rods I had made to order. Mine's got a little more flex to it than Margaret Mary's. I carry three hundred yards of twelve-pound test monofilament, and I got Margaret Mary's loaded up with about two hundred yards of twenty-five-pound test. I tell you, two years ago this little gal couldn'ta fought a crappie with a twelve-ton winch, but today she got that big albacore slick as you please. I'm fixing to cut her tackle down some."

"Lose much tackle today?" Guy asked.

"Eight or ten rigs. Got into some big dolphin that took some of it, and big 'cuda took the rest. Romeo, you get somebody to get the meat off that snapper and put it on the cold and we'll take it on back with us tomorrow evening. You can do what you want with the rest of the fish."

"Thank you very much, sar," Romeo said, grinning.

Bert got up on the dock and, speaking as though Romeo weren't there, said, "These people sure go for fish. And they don't get enough when they got to work all day like now. Romeo, how about you rinse off the tackle and set it in the dock house for me for the morning. Then you tell John to bring us a couple of bourbon to the room. There's anything I like it's fishing all day and then sticking my head out of a hot shower ever once in a while to nibble on a bourbon."

Lights had gone on all over the house. As we walked up the path I could hear the slap of small waves, the distant humming rumble of the generator house, the whine of a mosquito next to my ear.

The pool lights were on. There were just two people left by the pool, Port Crown and Puss McGann. I saw Crown tilt his seamed face at the darkening sky and heard the bray of his laugh. I saw Puss slap at her leg and then they got up and started slowly toward the main house.

People settled down on the shadowy veranda, in the main lounge and living room, or in the adjacent play room closer to the bar. Guy Brainerd had detached Bridget. After I got a drink, I slanted over, subtle as a moose, to the side of Cam Duncan who was watching Bonny Carson poke through the record cabinet.

"This is some layout, Mr. Duncan."

"One of the ground rules is no last names on the island, Sam."

"So be it. Are you Cam?"

"For Cameron. Cameron Mackenzie Duncan. You're right about Dubloon Cay, Sam. It is some layout. Mike knew exactly what he wanted, and the only way he could get the island was to take it on a ninety-nine-year lease agreement with her Majesty's Government. It hurts me to think he doesn't own it, but he tells me he is going to have damn little interest in what will happen to it eighty-nine years from now. That's when it runs out. I can see what he means."

"How does he keep in touch with what's going on while he's here?"

"That's one of the functions of the incredible Fletcher Bowman. Mike had a ham radio installation put in. Fletcher has an FCC license and a limey license, and every night he gets in touch with Ralph Pegler on Mike's New York staff who has his ham station up at his home in Connecticut, and Mike is up to date on all catastrophes."

"Have you been working for Mike a long time?" I asked. It was a pretty leaden-footed question, and I think it amused him.

"Not long. A couple of years now. I'm a tax attorney, of the new breed of specialist's specialist, a corporation tax attorney. Mike has another kind of specialist on the personal tax questions, a bright boy named Dave McGinty. Dave is involved in a practically perpetual audit of Mike's current affairs by the Bureau. Mike is in a bracket that calls for an automatic audit each year, and each year the return weighs about three pounds, so it takes most of the year to get through it. I don't think Mike has the faintest damn idea of what he's worth, and I don't think anybody else does either. If anybody could make a close guess, it would be Amparo Blakely."

"Speak of the devil," said Amparo Blakely softly at my elbow.

"The question of the hour," Cam said, "is what is Mike worth?"

"I didn't bring it up," I said.

She smiled at me. Even in her low heels she was almost six feet tall. "I didn't think you did, Sam. I'll give you an answer, Cam. Mike is worth a good deal of money sometimes. Other days he's hardly worth anything. It all depends."

Cam said, "Anything you want to know about Mike, just ask Amparo. She's the perfect confidential secretary. She won't even tell you what time it is by Mike's clock."

"Oh, poo! Cam, I worry about you. You ought to put some weight on. You're a rack of bones, actually. It would take three of you to make one of Sam."

"I like to have you worry about me," he said. They smiled at each other with obvious affection. She stood close enough to me so that I got more of the physical impact of her. She was built to my scale. She outweighed Cam and looked perfectly capable of snapping his spine with her thumbs, but that did not make her look less feminine. She was of the female persuasion, brushed, scrubbed, scented, and packed tightly and pneumatically into her bronzy hide.

"You shouldn't look so worn and frail, Cam," she said.

Cam looked beyond her and said, "I am not so frail but what I feel a basic urge to tweak the place where those green shorts of the lady editor are the tightest."

Amparo turned and looked and said, "Go ahead, darling. I dare you. They look slightly fraudulent. I pray to God we're not into a new age of fundamental falsies."

"Murphy called that rear elevation saucy," I said.

"And saucy it is," Amparo said. "Our Miss Hallowell has a nice way with words. Elda Garry is, I am afraid, not entirely oblivious to the general impression created. Try a tweak, Cameron. Think of it as character analysis. Maybe she'll go seven feet into the air and give a hoarse cry of anguish."

"Or lust. That would be worse," Cam said. "I don't think I could adjust to that."

"It would give her such a pretty problem though. Mike is Guy's valued client. What happens to the valued contract if Guy's favorite lady editor makes a scene over a gesture of affection on the part of one of Mike's bright young lawyers?"

"She looks as though she could make her decision in midair and come down with her script all planned," Cam said.

"Poor Guy," Amparo said. "He seems to be inevitably and fatally attracted to tailored women who jangle. But I'm afraid we're talking out of school in front of Sam. Sam, we're both fond of Guy and you would be too if you could know him. He's a very sincere man, and he has a genius touch for public relations. But he has foul taste in women, and each new one breaks his heart, and this one is just a bit more grim that the last two or three."

"Now?" Cam asked.

"You really mean it, you wretch! All right. Now."

Cam winked owlishly and strolled over to where Elda Garry stood talking with Bundy and Jack Buck and Warren Dodge, laughing her silvery and shimmering laugh at them, inundating them with her fashionable little restaurant chatter.

Cam edged in beside her, between her and Warren, and put his arm casually around her narrow waist. Amparo and I watched intently. We saw her stiffen and attempt to pull away and glance around at where Guy stood talking with Bridget. But Cam blithely hauled her back and she apparently decided to suffer the unexpected embrace. Then Cam's thin hand slid down and, deliberately, emotionlessly, callously, he caught a tender roundness of flesh between thumb and finger and pinched and twisted at the same time. Elda Garry went up onto her toes and took a quick half step toward little Bundy, then recovered herself and turned sharply and stared at Cam. He gave her his ugly and amiable smile. It seemed almost possible to hear the little chromed gears meshing in the sleek blond head. She glanced at Guy again, and glanced at Mike Dean as he came into the room in his Basque shirt and black Bermuda shorts, and brought her eyes back to Cam. And added it all up and gave him a pointy little smile and leaned closer and said something half under her breath. In a few minutes Cam came back to us.

"You are a foul rascal," Amparo said, laughing.

"It's all real," Cam said. "And taut as a winter apple. You're the analyst, Miss Blakely. As soon as she decided not to go up in smoke, what did she say to me?"

Amparo frowned and pursed her lips and looked at the floor for a few moments. "Hmmm. Something like, 'You are a naughty, naughty man.' Right?"

He shook his head. "You kill me, Amparo. I wouldn't have minded a close guess, because it's pretty obvious the *kind* of thing she would say. But you hit it precisely on the button, and that almost alarms me."

"We're not always like this, Sam," Amparo said. "Just when we get down here to the island. Then all the shoes come off and the hair is let down."

"You shook me up with that idea about falsies," Cam said. "After suggesting a horror like that, I was forced to go check it out. Everybody is empty, and the bar is yonder."

We went into the play room. I had been hearing the sound of table tennis for several minutes. Tommy McGann was playing with a young girl. She was quick and slim and dark, and her hair was in long braids. She was dark as any gypsy, teeth flashing white in her face, lips painted a burgundy red. She wore a red off-the-shoulder blouse and pink skin-tight pants that came slightly below the knee and were laced with black at the sides.

"Is that the Crown girl?" I asked Amparo.

"That's Lolly. I envy the resilience of the young, Sam. At three she got so potted I didn't think she'd be able to find her room. Port was very annoyed with her. And now look at her."

After we put in the drink order, I turned and watched her. She seemed to be giving Tommy a close battle. Tommy won, twenty-one to sixteen, then Puss McGann and Jack Buck joined them in doubles, Jack and Puss against Tommy and Lolly. Jack Buck was the poorest player, but Puss was, by a considerable margin, the best. When Lolly was not smiling her face had a sullen look. Her young breasts were sharp against the red blouse. Jack Buck had the square face and the yellow brush cut of any Navy recruiting poster. But he did not manage to look like a clean cut young man. He looked like a dogged and somewhat dangerous young man. There was a knife tattooed on his right forearm, with a snake writhing around it. His gray eyes were slightly undersized and there was a hint of brutality around his mouth. I decided that were I Porter Crown, I would not take my rebellious daughter on a prolonged cruise with Jack Buck.

The meal was served buffet style. The food was abundant and excellent. I wound up eating with Bridget, Amparo and Mike Dean at a table in the corner of the living room. Mike Dean ran the conversation like a train. Bridget and Amparo were the straight men. They fed him the right lines at the right times. Mike told the history of his looking around for a hideaway, and all the misadventures before he finally had it the way he wanted it. It was entertainingly told and in spots it was funny as hell. Mike made himself the stupid and innocent victim of all kinds of ludicrous mistakes, including one narrow mistake of nearly building on the wrong island. It was all much fun; and when the meal was over I wasn't one millimeter closer to knowing anything at all about Mike Dean.

After dinner Mike and Fletcher Bowman disappeared, and I guessed they were in their habitual nightly communication with the man in Connecticut. The bar was open. There was a fine moon. There was high fidelity music and dancing on the shadowy veranda, for those who cared to. Guy Brainerd, Porter and Tessy Crown and Cam Duncan played bridge.

Bonny Carson had taken over the record player. She selected a lot of old stuff. And she would sit there on the floor, legs crossed, eyes shut, swaying back and forth and singing the lyrics without making a sound, her highball glass handy beside her.

I danced with Puss McGann. I had never danced with her before. It was precisely what I had expected. Dancing is supposed to have sexual overtones and implications. Puss turned it into an exercise as sterile as tennis. She moved gracefully and correctly and followed well, but I could have been dancing with a sister. When Tommy and Puss danced, aside from the fact she was a little too tall for him, they were of almost professional talent. And Tommy danced very well indeed with Lolly Crown. She was smaller, and she seemed to fit his arms better than Puss did. I saw her watching them while they danced. She wore a slightly wistful expression.

Dancing with Bridget was very pleasant indeed. She was a little warm and wavery with drink, but not too much so. She had an annoying tendency to hum the melody slightly off key, but that was all right too because she smelled good and felt good and was warm against me, and her face in the moving shadows was astonishingly pretty. Warren Dodge was gone. I was surprised he had lasted as long as he had. During the day he had taken on enough liquor to drop a moose in its tracks. Little Bundy kibitzed the bridge game, turning every ten seconds to look at Bonny Carson in a worried way. I wondered if he was trying to count her drinks. I watched Jack Buck dance with Tessy Crown, and there was a certain flavor about their dancing that made me wonder whether old Port was being stupid about his daughter or about his wife. I guessed Jack Buck at about twenty-eight, and Tessy somewhere in the ripeness of her thirties. Jack Buck was closer to her in age than Port in his early sixties.

I found Louise on a big settee on the veranda and

I asked her if she would dance. I had not danced with
her before. She butted her cigarette and stood up
obediently and came into my arms. Though she had
that look of almost-tallness, she was not tall. I often
have a great deal of difficulty dancing with women
her size, particularly the ones who seem to feel awkward unless they can stab you in the side of the
throat with their chin. But Louise had a sweet and
easy and natural grace. She was feathery and lithe
in my arms, tender and vulnerable and curiously
precious. When the long record ended I said, "That
was nice."

"I was afraid you'd be too tall. You're not. Why do
so many big men move so lightly?"

"There's a breeze now and it ought to keep the
bugs off the dock."

We walked down to the dock. There were mosquitoes in the grass, but when we were on the dock the
wind from the northeast was stiff enough to keep
them away. From the dock we could see the moon
three quarters full back over the house. The silver
moonlight made the house lights look orange. We
climbed into the cockpit of the *Try Again* and sat
in the two fishing chairs and I lighted our cigarettes.
We were better than two hundred feet from the
house and the music came down sweetly to us, nos-
talgic. When I looked at her the moonlight was so
bright on her still face that I could see that she was
crying, making a private matter out of it, crying
without a sound.

"Louise."

"I'll be all right in a minute."

"Want to talk about it?"

After a long pause she said, "No," so quietly I
barely heard it. I wanted her to talk about it and yet
I didn't. I wanted her to talk because then she would
be closer to me. But I also wanted her to be loyal
to him in spite of what he was, because it is a cheap
thing and a destructive thing in any marriage to

spill your bitterness and pain and resentment all over someone else. And I thought that if she confided in me, she might end up resenting me.

When her tears were over we talked casually about things of no importance, and then she said she thought she would go to bed. I got onto the dock and gave her my hand and pulled her up with just a bit too much energy so that she staggered against me. I put my hands on either side of her face, thumbs near the corners of her eyes, fingers in her dark hair. I looked down at the quiet face. Her eyes were unreadable pockets of a shadow. I kissed her gently and her lips were cool and unresponsive. Then I released her. She turned and walked away from me. I watched her. At the path she turned and walked at an angle across the lawn to one of the doors on the right wing of the veranda. She disappeared from the moonlight into the shadows.

I sat on the edge of the dock for a long time, and then I went to bed.

FOUR

I AM CURSED by an inability to sleep later than six-thirty in the morning. I put on swimming trunks and a gray sports shirt and took a towel with me to the pool. When I climbed out the girl named Booty came from the house in her white uniform and, wearing a shy and grave half smile, asked me if I would like my breakfast by the pool, and what would I like. When the juice and easy-over eggs and bacon and coffee were laid out on the metal table under the umbrella it looked like a Kodachrome ad for breakfast.

The Bufords joined me when I was on my second cup of coffee. They were ready for another day of fishing the flats. I asked him about the land development, and he went on and on about it. There were fourteen thousand acres, twenty natural lakes. It was called Lakeshore Gardens, and by God, it was the biggest and best development Florida had ever had. They'd put up four hundred homes already, and by the time they were through it would be a city of thirty or forty thousand people, with schools, city services, outdoor movies, shopping centers, the whole shooting match.

Booty brought me more coffee after they left, and soon Louise joined me. She wore a pink swim suit with black ruffles at the bodice. You couldn't have told from the way she acted that last night had ever happened. "Sam, has Mike Dean said anything to you about talking business?"

"Only that we'd get around to it sooner or later."

"Suppose they arrange to talk to us separately?"

"That would be okay. But I would like your word that you won't sign anything until we've talked it over together."

"I'm agreeable to that."

"This isn't anything like I thought it would be," Louise went on. "It's a little confusing. All these weird people. Did you hear the horrible fight in the night?"

"I didn't hear a thing."

"It was on the veranda. Men yelling at each other and a woman crying. Warren was snoring so loud I couldn't understand what it was all about. But I think the woman was Bonny Carson and one of the men was Fletcher Bowman. It was about three o'clock. Then some doors slammed and it was over."

"There're all the ingredients here for a lot of trouble."

"What are the plans for the day?"

"First find out if Mike wants to talk business. If not, I want to try some fishing."

"Tommy is going to do some skin diving."

"Amid the barracuda?"

"He says they won't bother anybody."

"Is he sure they have the word?"

"You know Tommy. He probably half hopes one will make a pass at him."

"How about fishing from the shore with me if we're not required around here?"

She hesitated for a moment and then agreed. I borrowed her sun lotion and used it liberally while she swam up and down the pool. There weren't very many early risers in the group. It was nearly quarter of nine before Fletcher Bowman put in an appearance. He wore brief knit trunks and had a striped towel around his neck. He was well browned and impressively muscled. He wore his All-American smile, and I was certain the label in the trunks would be a good one.

After he had sat with us and told us what a beautiful day it was, and how many gallons of water the pool held and how the purifying plant worked, he said, "I do hope you people weren't upset in any way by the little disturbance we had in the wee hours."

"I heard it," Louise said, "but Sam slept through it and so did Warren. I don't know about the others. What was it about?"

He looked uneasy for the first time since I had met him. "It was a little shabby, I'm afraid. Poor Bonny Carson was completely and suddenly drunk. I don't think she knew where she was or what her name was. Let's say she is at a . . . difficult transition place in her life. She and Mike have been friends for years. Now she wants Mike's backing for a new musical. He doesn't think she ought to try it. We don't think much of the book or the songs, and he's afraid of what a flop might do to her. But no decision has been made as yet. Anyway, that's just background. That young Jack Buck got just tight enough to decide to take Bonny to her bed, probably so he could brag about it later. She certainly wasn't in any condition to provide anything but acquiescence. Bundy took objection to the plan. Jack knocked him down. Bundy came and woke me up and we intercepted them outside Bonny's room. By then she was having a crying jag. Jack was ugly about it, but I broke it up. If Port Crown wasn't such a stubborn man, Jack Buck would be gone long ago. But Jack is the son of some old rancher buddy of Port's who died broke, and Port thinks Jack is a fine virile young man. I think he's a punk with a mean streak. Were I Port, I would no more travel with Jack and my wife and daughter than I'd stick my arm in a snake pit. After Jack went out last night to sleep aboard the *Portess,* I sat on the veranda for a half hour to make certain he wouldn't try again. Enough of that. I hope we won't have any more of that sort of thing. What are your plans for today?"

"We've been waiting to see what Mr. Dean has in mind," I said.

He gave me a quick look of disapproval. "Mike and I have been going over a few things with Cam Duncan this morning. I asked him when we ought to have our little meeting about the Harrison Corporation and he said there was no rush about it. I gathered from that he doesn't want to bring it up today. In fact, Mike and Port and Cam and I are going out in the *Try Again* at nine-thirty. We're taking lunch with us and we'll be back about four-thirty. I wish we could take more, but four is about the maximum for comfort and good fishing. I talked to Tommy last night. Tomorrow he and Puss are going out on the *Try Again* with Mike and Amparo. Warren wasn't interested. Maybe the next day you and Sam could go, Louise?"

There was a little needle in the offer, very subtle, but sharp enough. "Sam and I are going to do some fishing today," she said.

"From the shore," I said. "How about tackle?"

"There's more than enough in the dock house. Just take what you think you need and rinse it in fresh water before you put it back. If you go east up the beach to where the rocky point is, there's supposed to be good fishing there. Wear something on your feet. Those rocks are jagged."

We saw the *Try Again* off at nine-thirty, wished them luck and waved to them as they sped out of the bay. A sleepy Bridget walked down with Tommy and Puss to help us wave them off.

"Hung?" I asked her.

"Not too terribly. Something keeps going sort of bong bong right between my eyes. But I've got the remorses about running off at the mouth. To you and other people. Was I completely horrible?"

"Just gay," I said, grinning at her.

"My God, you look bigger undressed than you do dressed. Sam the moose."

"Don't hurt his feelings," Puss said. "He's very sensitive. Say, what are you kids going to do after breakfast?"

"Me," said Bridget, "me, I'm going to slob around in the sun and try to forget I should be inside at the good old Olivetti Studio 44, pecking out something deathless about our host for the lady editor."

"And I'm going to see if I can spear something," Tommy said.

"We've had breakfast and we're going up the beach to fish," Louise said. "You want to come along, Puss?"

"Three's a crowd," she said. "Oops, that doesn't sound right. Anyhow, Tommy makes me so nervous I have to watch the water and keep wringing my hands until he bobs up again."

"I wish I could have brought my compressor and my air tanks," Tommy said wistfully. "I can stay down about two and a half minutes, but what good is that?"

We went into the little dock house. Rods rested on wall pegs. I picked out two spinning rods and reels that looked sturdy, piled some lures, swivels, leader wire, a pair of rusty pliers and a sharp but rusty knife in a battered aluminum box, and we headed up the beach. The beach was sandy, but the shallow water just off shore was full of dark rocks. A half mile from the little bay the sand ended and we had to walk over gray-black, water-eroded rocks. The rocky area became wider. It had a lost and fearsome look, like part of a destroyed planet. We had to keep looking ahead to pick out the flat places. There were windows of conch shells, tossed high on the rock by tide and winds. The sun had whitened them, and they were like the bones of the dead in a barren world.

Louise stopped and made a sweeping gesture with her arm and said, "Just look at it, Sam!" I saw what she meant. The scrub was vivid green on our right. The black-gray tortured rock was a fifty-yard strip between the green of the leaves and the streaked blue and tan and green and yellow of the water.

I found us a place on a point where we stood six feet above the water. I rigged the rods and showed her how to handle spinning tackle. After three casts she had the knack of it and began to get the yellow feathered dude out to a respectable distance. There were no fish left in the world. There was not even a knock. Two vultures dipped to take a closer look at us, and then sailed away, rising effortlessly on the wind currents.

I realized Louise had stopped casting. I looked at her and she was looking farther up the shoreline.

"What is it?"

"Isn't that Skylark up there?"

I looked. The boy was two hundred yards away, kneeling on the rocks, looking down into the water. I saw him yank something small and silvery out of the water. We folded our futile tent and walked up to him. He grinned at us. The water right next to the rocks was black and roiled with a dense school of menhaden minnows. The school was twenty feet long and ten feet wide. Skylark was dangling a small bare bright hook in the school and rolling the line back and forth between thumb and finger to spin the hook. The minnows, three and four inches long, would bite at the bare hook and he would yank them out and drop them in a small tide pool behind him. He had over a dozen in the pool, scurrying around busily.

"Do you eat those?" I asked him.

"Oh, no. No, I will show you." He put the small hook and line aside and picked up a heavy line with a large hook. He hooked a live minnow through the back and swung it around his head several times and threw it out about forty feet. I swear it wasn't out there ten seconds before something gulped it down. Skylark set his hook and brought the fish in, hand over hand. It was a five-pound yellowtail, and he carried it over and put it in a pool shaded by the rocks. There were two other yellowtails and about a ten-pound albacore in the pool.

He told us to go ahead and use his minnows. We hesitated perhaps one hundredth of a second. Two hours never passed more quickly. My drag was set too tight, and the first stunning, breathtaking rush of a barracuda broke the line. At one point, after an hour of it, I was going after another minnow when I heard Louise yelp and I turned and looked at her. Her barracuda jumped and it was a big one, bigger than any I had hooked thus far. I watched her. She stood in that pink suit on a flat-topped rock with the blue water beyond her. She stood braced on her slim and perfect legs, her hair glossy in the sun. She fought the big fish and the smooth muscles bunched under the velvetiness of her back. The reel whined when he'd make a run, and when he'd try to rest for another run and another jump, she would work him and talk to him. She was brightly and intensely alive. "Oh, come along now, you monstrous darling. Come to Louise. Oh, be a good boy, be a honey pie. Whoa! No more of that, pretty baby. Come on, pretty baby. I won't give you an inch, not an inch."

And as she tired the fish, I looked at her and I knew that this was the way I wanted her to be. This was the way she had to be. To have her alive again made my eyes sting. That was the precise moment when I knew I loved her. I had known I wanted her. But I thought it was just wanting. But it was more. I could hide the wanting and never do anything about it. But this I knew that I would not be able to hide. This I knew I would do something about.

The weary fish came in with docile reluctance. Ten feet from the rocks he made his last effort. He surged half out of the water and shook his frightful snaggled jaws, and made a short run of perhaps twenty feet. She walked carefully along the rocks to

a flat place where a rock slanted down into the water
at a shallow angle, rod bent sharply, tugging the
fish along. I went down onto the rock and took hold
of the brass swivel and, pulling on the leader, horsed
the four and a half feet and about sixty pounds of
him all the way out of the water. He had the true
grin of the barracuda. He kept opening and closing
his mouth. The snaggly teeth were monstrous. Louise
came down beside me and put her hand on my arm
and we looked at him. He was breathing heavily, like
a tired and dying man.

The barracuda is not a foulness. He is as clean and
functional as a rapier. He is no scavenger. He eats
nothing that is not trying to get away from those
jaws in haste and terror. He can lie like a spent
torpedo in the water and, with one movement, he can
be gone as though he had never been.

"Do you want him, Skylark?" I asked the boy.

"No. I will smash his head with a stone and get
the hook."

"No," Louise said. "Don't do that."

I looked at the savage eye and knew what she
meant. I bent and clipped the leader a cautious
distance from those jaws. Using the rod butt I nudged
him back into the water. He had been out of the
water a long time. He rolled onto his back and completely over and onto his back again several times.
He found equilibrium, hung poised a few inches
under the surface, gill plates spreading widely each
time he sucked water. And then he swam very slowly
along the shore and through the minnow school. A
lane opened for him as they fled in panic. And he
turned out toward deep water and we could not see
him any more. The hook in his jaw would corrode
and separate.

We went back from the water and sat on a rock
and smoked and talked about the fish. I kept trying
to keep that quality of excitement alive in her.
Her hands were shaky from the long exertion and

she massaged her right wrist. But the glow was fading too quickly, and she was becoming muted and remote again.

She looked at me and pressed her fingertip against my upper arm. It left a white impression against the burn that lasted a full second.

"You've had enough."

"I can take a little more."

"I'll just watch, I think. I don't want to catch a littler fish than him. Not today anyway."

She came down and watched. I lost a wildly leaping and gyrating needle fish, and I caught two more yellowtails to add to Skylark's hoard, and then I got a better fish that felt like a yellowtail. He was struggling as I slowly brought him in, and then he went curiously slack. There was still something on the line, but it did not feel heavy. I brought in the head of a large yellowtail, gill plates still working.

"Barracuda," Skylark said.

Had it been whole it would have been the largest yellowtail we had caught that day. It had been slashed in half, and so keen had been the teeth, so powerful the jaws, that I had felt no jerk or tug as eight to ten pounds of living fish had been cut free. I looked at it and then looked at Louise. Her eyes were round and she swallowed hard and said, "When I thought of them biting I didn't . . ."

"I know what you mean."

And that was enough. It was after twelve. We threaded the fish on a stick. Skylark carried one end and I took the other. Louise carried the gear. After we took the fish to the kitchen, I went back to the dock and found that Louise had rinsed the gear and put it away. I went to my room and showered. My back and my legs felt hot. Just as I pulled on fresh shorts there was a knock at the door. I opened it and John handed me a planter's punch and said, "Mrs. Dodge said to bring this, sar."

I thanked him. I sipped at it as I finished dressing.

It was cold, tart and good. I realized it had been a
long time since I had been able to loaf. It shocked me
that I had put all the problems of Harrison so firmly
out of my mind. I had a hunch I was going to be a
whirlwind when I got back.

As I went onto the veranda, my sports shirt felt
itchy against the burn on my back and shoulders.
Warren was sitting in front of the lounge smoking a
cigar. I could hear a table tennis game going. I could
see a group out by the pool.

"What's the deal on lunch?" I asked Warren.

"I wouldn't know and I wouldn't care. I just had
breakfast, buddy." He was surly and he looked ill.

"Tommy do any good with his spear?"

"I wouldn't know that either, buddy."

I shrugged and walked away from him. Puss was
by the pool. She said she and Tommy had taken a
skiff out to a reef and Tommy had speared a couple
of big grouper. I asked for a second punch. Louise
joined us and I thanked her for sending the first one.
Lunch was served by John and Booty at one-thirty,
on the veranda or by the pool, take your choice.
Bonny Carson still wasn't up. Amparo, Tessy Crown,
Lolly Crown and Elda Garry ate at the pool-side,
a hen party for four. I didn't need any more sun. I
ate on the veranda with Guy Brainerd, Bridget,
Tommy and Puss.

I felt so drugged by the sun and drinks that right
after lunch I went back to my room, stripped down
to my shorts and lay on top of the spread. I left the
room door to the veranda open for the sake of the
breeze. I had noticed that it was hard to look through
the screen into the dim room and see anybody. There
was a flavor of siesta in the air. I guessed that most
of the others had folded, too. I knew that Tommy and
Puss and Louise had.

I tried to anticipate how Mike Dean would handle
it when he got around to it, and that kept me awake
just long enough so that I was not quite asleep when

I was disturbed by the small pinging noise of the spring on my screen door.

I rocked up onto my elbow and squinted at Bridget silhouetted in the open doorway.

"You decent?" she said in a half whisper.

"Come on in."

She shut the door quietly and came over and sat on the foot of the bed, facing me. I moved my legs to make room for her. She lighted two of her cigarettes and handed me one. She seemed to be intensely amused at something.

"Oh, my God," she said.

"What is it?"

"Excuse me for barging in on you, but I wanted to tell this little nugget to somebody and I couldn't wait and you are the one I thought of. Why is that? Do people always come and tell you stuff? Is it because you don't do an awful lot of jabbering yourself? Or maybe people just get a feeling about you that you won't blab."

"I've wondered myself," I said.

"Don't sound so grumpy. All you were going to do is sleep. Did you notice how grouchy sincere ole Guy Brainerd was at lunch?"

"I guess I did."

"And he ought to be happy as clams. He's in the other wing and the jauntiest little fanny of the class of '48 at Wellesley is in the next door room, all handy like. Anyway, right after lunch dear Elda said she wanted to talk to me in private. She came to my room. I thought she despised me. Maybe she still does. Anyway, she told me that she had thought I was sort of rattle-brained, but after knowing me she has realized how really wise and mature I am about people, and she wanted to know if I thought she was doing the right thing. I forgot just exactly what nauseous little euphemism she used, but she let it be known that she has been letting humble Guy enjoy the infinite pleasures of her incredibly desirable body for

lo these many moons. She came damn close to sim-
pering, which I honestly do not think I could have
taken. So what is your problem, darling, I say. She
beats her way around about eighteen bushes before I begin to get the message. It's simply that she
wants to marry him and so far he won't get off
the dime and start the legal wheels whirling, so she
is withdrawing her body fair until Guy jumps
through her hoop. She told him that last night and
it seems there was quite a scene, all in whispers, of
course. And she wrenched herself away from him
and locked herself in the bathroom and cried practically all night long. Do I think she is right?"

"What did you tell her?"

"I had to think fast. I have a hunch it might work,
and I couldn't let that happen. The present Mrs.
Brainerd is a bitch, but at least she keeps her nose
out of the office. This item would try to run our shop
and I think I like it there, and I think she would
run it into the ground. So I had to come up with
something that would shake her. She wasn't asking
my advice. Her mind was made up. She was just
staking out the limits of her own reservation and
putting up the no shooting and trapping signs. So I
came up with a doozey. I told her I thought it was
a terrible mistake. I told her I wouldn't mention any
names, but there was another woman in Guy's past,
a woman to whom he was strongly drawn physically.
I told her that she had saved him from that awful
woman. She had given him the strength to break the
ties of the flesh. And now, if she denied him, she
would be driving him right back into the arms of
the third woman."

"Very tricky," I said. "Appeal to the martyr in her."

"And also scare hell out of her. Which it did. It
worked." She laughed. Her eyes were dancing. "And
so right now lady bountiful is probably in Guy's bed,
saving him from himself. She had that look when

she loped off." And she laughed again, and all of a sudden she was crying.

"Hey!" I said. "Hey, now!"

She flung herself onto my chest and nuzzled her head into my throat and enough of the words were intelligible so I could piece it together: ". . . years older and bald-headed . . . so sincere and with that ridiculous chin. He'd never look at me. Never, never, never, no matter what I do. So damn foolish, all of it. Likes them slinky and bitchy and affected. Oh, damn it all."

So, incredibly, Bridget was in love with Guy Brainerd, and she had just sent Elda Garry trotting off to Guy's bed, and she had thought she could make a big scandalous joke about it, and laugh over it with a stranger, but it had cracked her up.

"Always the wrong guy," she said. "Always." And a tear dropped like wax on the side of my throat and she snuffled. I had my arm around her waist. And pretty soon I found I had to send my mind winging away to some place else. I thought desperately of the barracuda and of how many shares of Harrison Mike Dean controlled, and how I was going to present my beef to the union officials, and then I tried to replay an old football game, and then I tried multiplying numbers by twelve, and then I tried to visualize a tall pitcher of ice water. But a bed is a bed is a bed. And an armful of girl in sun suit is an armful of girl in sun suit and no matter how far away I threw my mind it came zooming back to the here and the now and the scent of the crisp fresh hair and the firm warmth against chest and against my arm. So as I was bracing myself to come surging up to a sitting position and put an abrupt end to all this dangerous nonsense, she turned her head a little and caught up a little bit of the hide on the side of my neck between her teeth and nibbled it very gently. It seemed as if her teeth made little holes and all good intentions and will power drained out through those little holes.

I hitched her around and found her mouth with mine. In a little while she got up and went over and closed the door and came back, dropped her halter top and her sun shorts to the floor beside the bed, stood there for not more than two seconds and then stretched out beside me.

She bent over the side of the bed and got her cigarettes out of the pocket of the sun shorts, lit two and gave me one and lay back in the circle of my arm, huffed out a big cloud of smoke and said, "Cheap and silly. A blond bawd in bed. I despise myself, ole Sam. Why use you to try to get even with the game?"

"It depends on how you look at it."

"Nobody ever gets even. My God, I wish I could be like this. I wish I could be blithe and gay about it, and pay no attention to it, and indulge in it with big handsome strangers just for the sake of the pleasure, which, I might add, was considerable, and I do thank you, sir."

"There isn't much to the people who can toss it off like that and go on their way. Jaded little empty people, Bridget."

She sighed. "I wish I didn't have to hurt so much and feel so cheap and bitchy and reckless, and hate myself. You see, it's this damn active conscience I've got. The way I was brang up, I guess."

"Don't feel bad about it this time. You didn't plan it."

"I don't even know if I did or I didn't. With you it's the dark one, Louise, isn't it?"

"How did you know?"

"The way you look at her. And I saw you on the dock last night. It gave me a lump in the throat, kind of."

"Yes, with me it's that dark one."

"I think she's one of the two or three really beautiful women I've ever seen." She lifted her long and rounded left leg, the leg next to me, and locked her knee and pointed her toes at the ceiling. "Every five minutes my thighs get heavier. They're getting all nasty and meaty. In one more year I'll be round as a barrel."

"Fishing?"

"I guess to hell I am. So if I'm fishing, Sam'l, build me up."

"The thighs are not nasty and meaty. They are beautiful. They are delights. A man could stand on the corner of Fifth and Fifty-Second for weeks at a time without ever seeing a pair of thighs that . . ."

"Don't overdo it, Buster," she said, dropping her leg. "What's with the slob husband of the dark one? Just a plain and simple nogudnik? Just an All-American slob?"

"Completely."

"So why doesn't she ditch him? She's the one with the money, no?"

"It's complicated. Her father had a hell of a heavy hand. She fought him every inch of the way, standing and slugging toe to toe. It gave her a funny kind of emotional insecurity and, after he died, a curious guilt complex. I think that if he had lived, she would have divorced Warren six months after they were married. But she seems to feel some ethical and emotional obligation to make this impossible marriage work. Tommy fought his old man in a different way. He just got out, just as soon as he could."

"He's a doll. Luck in your venture, Sam. I wish you more luck than I'm going to have."

She sat up and put the halter top on, and then stood up and pulled the shorts on and zipped them at the side. She leaned over the bed and kissed me lightly on the lips and pulled back not over an inch and, looking directly into my eyes, said, "If I don't get around to saying it sometime, you are a nice guy, Glidden. And if I can get over feeling like a cheap bitch, maybe I'll find out this did me good."

She opened the door cautiously, stood listening, then pushed the screen open and went out. She waved at me through the screen and then she was gone.

I fell asleep as abruptly as if I'd tumbled into a hole.

FIVE

IT IS A RARE THING for me to see something that physically sickens me. It has happened only three or four times in my life, and it is always unexpected.

I didn't expect anything like that to happen during what was left of Thursday when I woke up at three-thirty. The interval of sleep had made the episode of Bridget seem completely unreal. It was more like something I had dreamed than something that had happened. But there were the two lipsticked butts in the glass ash tray and one medium long blond hair on the pillow. I drew it between my thumb nail and fingernail and it coiled into a tight coppery spring.

I felt sweaty so I showered again, inspected my sunburn and decided I hadn't overdone it, and got dressed. The veranda was empty, the main lounge was empty. Warren Dodge was alone in the play room with a dark highball and a copy of *Time*. He glanced up and looked back at the magazine. I was surprised he didn't move his lips when he read. His underlip was strikingly pendulous.

Bonny Carson lay prone in the sun by the pool. Bundy sat under the shade of an umbrella, playing solitaire and listening to a transistor portable set at low volume. The place was still in the grip of siesta. I found John and he found me a cold beer. I felt mildly restless and decided I might as well take a look at the generator house. The path was winding. When I stopped to drink beer out of the bottle I would pick up a mosquito or two. I came to a clearing about two hundred yards behind the house. The busy noise of the generators seemed to come from a building on the far side of the clearing. There was a tumbledown shack on my left, set back against the pines and palmetto scrub. One of the two porch posts was gone and the porch roof had a drunken sag. After I had walked past it I glanced back at it. I stopped and turned, frowning and puzzled. Porter Crown's continental wife stood in an attitude that was both furtive and rigid, staring into a broken window. Her red hair was flame against the weathered gray of the wood. She no longer looked sleepy and unresponsive. She was wearing gold slacks and a black blouse. She should not have worn slacks. Her hips were too abundant, her body, though attractive, too billowing and soft. She seemed to be peering into one corner of the window, so as not to be seen. I wondered what the hell was going on. I was not more than twenty feet from her, but she did not know anyone was within nine miles. I had half decided it was none of my business, and I was about to turn and be on my way when some sixth sense warned her. She snapped around and looked toward me. In that unguarded moment her face was a shocking mask of evil, the eyes slitted, the mouth loose. I could see that she was breathing heavily. Within moments her face reassumed its habitual dull and sleepy expression and she moved away from the window and walked, quite slowly, toward the path that led back to the house.

I matched a mental coin and shrugged when I lost and went stealthily to the window anyway. They were in sunlight that came down through the broken roof. They were on a pile of straw. Her skirt and his trousers were in a heap beside them. I saw the knife and snake tattooed on his forearm. They plunged and strained as I watched. I was frozen there, but I do not think it could have been for more than three or four seconds. The eyes of Lolly Crown were squeezed tight against the sunlight, and her face was corroded by passion, her mouth savage and ugly with it. I sensed she had rot and evil wisdom in her far beyond her years. I turned away. I was not sickened by seeing a fragment of the sex act. That was merely slightly ludicrous, as it always is to anyone but the participants. What actually physically sickened me, in retrospect, was the memory of the voyeur expression on the face of Tessy Crown as she had watched the hired hand and her gypsy step-daughter, the memory of evil seen as clearly as anyone can ever hope to see it.

I walked back toward the house. I felt as if I might gag. I finished the beer and then, with a grunt of effort, I hurled the bottle high over the trees. It spun and twinkled in the sun. I felt as if I wanted a bath with yellow soap and a wire brush.

Tessy Crown sat on the far side of the pool from Bonny and Bundy, sat at a tin table under the shade of a striped umbrella. It was none of my damn business, I told myself. Stay the hell out of it, Glidden.

But I walked over and sat down with her without invitation and said, "Did you follow them?"

She gave me a torpid smile. "Too much zun makes me all bink and schleepy, yes?"

"Did you follow them?"

"On the boat I am so careful I don't get too much zun."

"Damn it, are you going to do anything about it? That's your step-daughter. You have an obligation."

The dozing pearly smile was unaltered. Her teeth were tiny and very white. Her breasts were vast. "But even zo, even in the shzade I get bink. From reflections, they tell me, but to me that does nod make sense."

I gave up. I went away. That was what she wanted me to do. And it still wasn't any of my damn business. I went down to the dock with a small group when the *Try Again* came in. They had a good catch, but nothing special. The Bufords came in a few minutes later and they too had an average catch. The Bufords cleaned up and, shortly after five, took off in the float plane with their fish and their tackle and their sunburn.

When I went inside Puss was sitting on the veranda talking to Lolly Crown. Lolly looked fresh and poised. I had the strong feeling that this little business vacation was jinxed. Nothing was going to go right. It seemed to be deteriorating rapidly, and I had the feeling that there were worse things ahead. And I had more than a vague gnawing of guilt about Bridget. The worst aspect of it seemed that it had happened with Louise only two rooms away.

That night, after dinner, Fletcher Bowman asked me to come to Mike Dean's room. I wished I had had four less drinks before dinner. I had drunk out of a feeling of depression. I felt fuzzy and dulled.

Mike's room was large. It was a corner room, with a space for a conversation group of tables and chairs. Mike kept kidding Bowman about the fish that had gotten away from him. I turned down a drink. Cam Duncan arrived a few minutes later.

"You people have me outnumbered," I said.

"There's nothing official about this, Sam," Mike said with a hurt look. "Just a little chatter." Cam made himself a drink. Bowman had made one for himself. Mike had his usual steaming cup of black coffee.

Mike settled himself in his chair, sighed and said, "I'll tell you one thing. You people did a good job of protecting yourself in the clinches. We'd hoped to control more than a hundred and eighty thousand shares by now. I won't try to kid you, Sam. You were the one who did the job. Dolson is a cipher, an empty desk chair."

"Gene Budler and I handled it. Al Dolson came up with some good ideas."

"You realize that where we stand now, we can force representation on the Board?"

"I suppose so. Whoever the Board is, I work for the Board. If they don't want me, I go to some other outfit."

"That's a healthy attitude," Mike said.

"Sure, and you can be a clown all your life," Cam Duncan said, grinning at me.

"What the hell does that mean?"

"You're only thirty, Sam," Cam said. "It's still going to take some time before you can work yourself up into a slot where you can get your hands on some stock option deals and make real money. And maybe by that time they will have slammed the door. You can't tell."

I began to sense the way it was going. "I don't need very much. Your people made a thorough investigation. You probably know I make twenty-five thousand."

"You're worth more," Mike said.

"I can get more. Some other place. But Harrison can't pay more. Not yet. Not for a while. Look, don't try to buy me. I live fine. I travel on expense account. I have a car and an apartment and all the clothes I need and I eat fine."

"We know most of the program you and Dolson have for Harrison," Bowman said. "Want to fill us in a little on it?"

I thought that over carefully. I knew the program was sound. I could see no harm in going ahead and telling them. It took me about ten minutes. God knows I'd said it enough times before. There was silence after I finished. They glanced at each other.

Bowman said, "What's your slant, Mike?"

Mike looked over my head and said softly, "I don't like it."

"What's wrong with it?" I demanded, getting hot.

Mike said, "Do you know the way some people drown? They try to swim after a boat in the wind.

For years Harrison was churning along and the boat was drifting farther and farther away. Now you want to put on a big spurt and catch it. But I don't think you will. I think you'll drown."

"But why?"

"You've got too heavy a tax burden, local, county and state. It'll get heavier. Wages are high and productivity is low. Your shipping costs are high. You can fix the rest of the wagon maybe, but you can't fix that part. Those items are beyond your control. Harrison was half asleep for too long, and the world moves too fast. You'll never take up all the slack and be in a healthy competitive position."

"I think we will. With a quality product plus top designing, people will pay just enough of a premium price to offset those factors we can't change."

"Will they?" Cam asked. "Are you sure?"

"That's not a fair question," Mike said. "Listen to me, Sam. Our little game up until now has gotten some national attention. In spite of the efforts of Guy Brainerd, the public seems to have a morbid interest in the activities of Mike Dean. Okay, suppose you keep the McGanns and the Dodges under your thumb. I may not be interested in putting a couple of men on the Board. I may give up on this thing and get out. So say you go along for five years, and at the end of that time you find out I was right, and Harrison folds. So where are you? By then you'll be thirty-five and you'll have wasted five years and worked your heart out for the chance of being associated with a big, loud failure. They'll remember you stood off Mike Dean and you lost."

"Or," said Cam Duncan smoothly, "look at the other side of the coin. Suppose you win. You won't hold a share of Harrison, and you won't have much savings after taxes. You win so that Warren Dodge can live high off the hog. That's about the face of it."

It was indeed very smooth.

"Suppose," I said, "you nail down the proxies you're

after. Another way to put it is to say I can't prevent them from signing after the snow job you do on them. Then what do you do?"

Mike shrugged. "We make our own survey. That loss record is pretty attractive, you know, in setting up a sale. I can think of a couple of outfits who might be interested."

"Even though you say the firm is doomed?"

"Maybe the buyer would be as optimistic as you are."

"So suppose a sale isn't feasible?"

"After our own survey," Bowman said, "we may come around to your way of thinking, Sam."

"Don't try to kid me. Why don't you level with me? With every trick you've been able to think of, what's your educated guess on how high you can bump the stock before the bottom falls out of it?"

Again they exchanged glances. Mike pursed his lips. "I employ some pretty good practical psychologists and some dandy statisticians and some bright accountants. The figure we come up with is fifty-four. That's the place to unload. It may not be the top, but it's the place where there'll be enough steam left in it to hold it up there while we unload."

I thought the figure over and heard myself whistle. Over two and a half millions for Louise alone if she got the word on the right timing. "With no beefs?" I asked them. "How about the SEC? How about the Justice Department?"

"Probably some beefs," Cam said. "Nothing that can't be handled. After the bottom falls out, there'll be some friends who will ride it down, and then we'll arrange for the sale to an outfit already lined up. With the right timing they'll get it at less than book, and be glad to get it. By then, of course, it will be off the big board."

"All this," I said, "is your second line of defense or something, after you make your survey."

"There's no need for sarcasm, Glidden," Mike said.

"You're not dealing with thieves or vandals. I make damn certain I operate within the law. I'd rather take the money out of Harrison than have it dribbled away over a period of years."

"How about the town? How about the employees?"

"I don't think this is the right time to sit around and bleed about that. There are all sorts of social agencies ready and anxious to step into such areas. And, after a time, there will be the inevitable adjustment, and everybody will be happy again," Bowman said.

"You can't make an omelette without breaking eggs," I said.

"I'd hoped you had a little more iron in you, Glidden," Mike said.

"Remember the rules of the island, Mike. You have to call me Sam, no matter how it hurts."

He flushed and then grinned. "At least you don't scare, even though you do sound a little bit Christer. When Harrison starts to climb it will be hotter than a pistol. People will be begging for it. We'll plant it in the scripts of a couple of television comics, make gags out of it."

"If I'm supposed to be bought, I'd like to know the price I'm bringing in the market place, Mike."

He went over to the writing desk, took something out of the drawer and handed it to me. I looked at the three documents. It didn't take long to get the picture. And they didn't play small, either. One was a contract form between me and Michael Davis Dean. He had already signed it. It was dated June second, the day after the Board meeting. It was a three-year employment contract at forty thousand a year. The second paper was a stock option agreement bearing the same date. I was entitled to buy ten thousand shares of Harrison Common from Mike Dean at eleven dollars a share. The third paper was a demand note on a New York bank with the figure left blank.

Mike said, "Will you excuse me and Fletcher for a while, Sam?" They left. I was alone with Cam Duncan. I wondered if they had sensed I felt more at ease with Cam and that, of the three, he was the only one I had found it possible to like.

"The note," he said, "is in case you need a little extra to pick up the stock."

"A big package deal. Where does the stock come from?"

"Mike's personal holdings of Harrison. You come in for a hundred and ten thousand and unload for five hundred and forty thousand on long-term capital gains. Then you'll have some capital to play with on other deals. I'm frank to admit, Sam, it gives me a little jealous itch. He hasn't thrown anything like that my way. By the end of three years you could damn well be far enough ahead of the game to retire."

"First I pinch myself, and then I ask what's the catch."

He took a sip of his drink. "Sam, when you watch the really big operators, there doesn't seem to be any rhyme or reason to what they do. They seem to make decisions on an emotional basis. You begin to think their shrewdness is just a myth. But over a period of time you can begin to see a pattern. Those papers were typed up this morning. Mike decided he wants you. He wants you on his personal staff. He doesn't haggle. He makes his top bid the first time."

"A third of a million dollars after taxes is a hell of a big bid. I feel shook, Cam."

He grinned. "I would too."

"And I can look at it another way. Through dummies and so on, he's picked up say a hundred thousand shares. And he stands to make three and a half million bucks. So what does it cost him to hedge his bet? Ten per cent of the take."

"It's not only hedging the bet. He, at the same time, is acquiring a hell of a competent man."

"Buying his soul?"

Cam gave me a sour look of annoyance and got up and paced over to the window to look down the slant of lawn toward the water. "Faustus is a little dated, Sam. You're a nice guy, but this is a practical world and you have to live in it. You've got to get the hell off your white horse or be left behind."

"I know all the rationalizations too. The world is insecure. Let me get mine first. They've given up the premium on decency."

He turned and the lamplight on his face emphasized the deep hollows in his cheeks. "Am I an indecent man?" he asked softly.

"Answer it yourself. Every man lives with himself. Every man shaves himself. And why the hell are we both feeling uncomfortable and slightly guilty right now just because I brought up the question of decency? What's turned it into a shameful subject?"

His smile was crooked. "I give you the pat answer. The decay of public morality, political morality, private morality. The venality of public institutions."

"So what you are saying to me, you and Mike Dean, is that these are the rules of the game, and it's time I accept the rules and make my pile. So it's a cynical invitation."

He sighed and collapsed into his chair. "You're a hell of a difficult man, Sam. I like you. I know what you're talking about. But I've outgrown my boyhood urge to fight windmills. Maybe you haven't. Take a good hard look at where you stand. I personally don't think Mike has to hedge the bet. I think he's going to acquire control anyway. And so do you. Suppose you stand on principle and refuse this offer. The Dean organization moves in. You go out on your ear, and in order to justify tossing you out, there'll be some publicity about a young, dreamy-eyed idealist who was so completely unsuited to running a big corporation that Mike had to bounce him in order to save everybody's marbles. And don't think that Guy Brainerd's mill won't grind that out in a way that will really sting."

"So?"

"So it's going to happen anyway. What do you do when a building is burning down? Do you paint safety slogans on the walls, or do you carry out the cash?"

"When do you want a decision?"

"There's no rush."

"There's no point in my carrying this stuff around. Here." He put it in the drawer. "Should I wait around for Mike to come back?"

"No. I'll tell him you're thinking it over."

I stood up and started toward the door and then turned back and said, "About this Bowman. Working with him would hardly be a joy."

"Mike makes optimum use of him. He makes optimum use of me. There's something to be said for being constantly stretched to fulfill your capacities. When you understand Fletcher he isn't so bad. He is just a completely and astonishingly emotionless man who has had to learn how to simulate warmth in order to get along."

I managed to get down to the dock without running into anybody. I went out toward the end to get away from the mosquitoes. I sat with my legs dangling. The fuzziness of the liquor was entirely gone.

Basically, what the hell did I owe anybody? By bucking Dean I was asking for five years of grueling, tense work, and the chance of success was smaller than it had seemed. Maybe getting away had given me some perspective. And there was a hell of a good chance that I wouldn't be able to buck him anyway. Louise was depressed and discontented. With the right urging, she'd sell out. Did I owe her anything? Or Tommy? Or Warren? Or Tom McGann, dead over two and a half years? Hadn't I fulfilled the promise I made him? I'd come back to Harrison, and I'd put in eight years, nearly. Was I supposed to sink with the ship, standing at attention, saluting the McGann banner?

And how about my duty to all those people who depend on the Harrison Corporation? Those poor desperate people who so delight in drawing eight hours' pay for two hours' work.

One third of a million bucks, plus forty thousand a year for at least three years, and probably a fatter contract when that one ran out.

Gene and Cary and Al were pulling for me. I'd had to stick my head in the lion's mouth, and they were hoping I'd give him a bad case of indigestion.

It wasn't as if I owned the company. I was just a hired hand.

Anybody else in the world would jump at it, Glidden. So what the hell is wrong with you? Scruples? It can't be so bad with Dean. Cam keeps his self-respect. It's a jungly world. A corporate entity is like a living creature. If it gets sick and wobbly, the other creatures bring it down and gorge on the fat.

Maybe I could sign up and talk Mike into doing it my way. Maybe, after I sign up, he'll be more willing to listen.

Stop kidding yourself, Glidden. Do yourself one little favor. Whatever you do, don't lie to yourself. It gets to be a habit.

I heard the sound of high heels on the dock. She was walking carefully, and silhouetted against the house lights.

"Sam?" she said.

"Right here, Louise."

She came and sat down beside me, close to me, and accepted a cigarette. "I understand there was a sort of a little conference tonight. I've been looking for you."

"How are things meanwhile back at the ranch?"

"Sticky. Little Bundy talked Bonny Carson into singing some of the numbers from the musical they want Mike to back. She's tight again and she went flat and we had to clap and everybody had horrid frozen smiles on their faces. Tommy and Lolly are having a desperate pingpong tournament. There's a poker game going—Mike and the Crowns and Cam and Guy

Brainerd and Amparo, with Elda looking on. Murphy or Bridget, or whatever you're supposed to call her, is in a corner of the lounge typing something. That Jack Buck person is being a charm boy with our Puss, filling her full of Texas talk. How did your conference go, Sam?"

I swear that I had intended to be completely honest with her, and tell her the details of the offer they made me.

"It was interesting," I said.

"I'll bet."

"Mostly I guess they just wanted to get my views on what I think can be done to make Harrison healthy. I gave them the three-star spiel."

"How did they take it?"

"It's hard to tell. They listened. Maybe I was wrong. Maybe Mike wants to do it my way. And, of course, that would give us better backing."

She took hold of my hand. "Sam, that's wonderful! Was that all?"

"That was all." The lie had a sick and sour taste. I'd taken my first Judas step. And I could see how the rest of it would go. Seriously, Louise, I see no harm in signing proxies over to Mike. Mike is a great guy. Very sound. You and Tommy sign the proxies and everything will be just dandy. Then he'll control two hundred and eighty out of four hundred and forty thousand shares, and your pal Sam Glidden is set for life.

Almost as though she had read my mind, she said, "I've decided to do whatever you recommend, Sam. You'll know what's best for Harrison. But . . ."

"But what?"

"I'd like to sell out and go away. I think that if Warren and I could go away alone, things might be different."

So, if that was what she wanted, I knew how it could be arranged.

There was a heavy stride on the dock. He came out

and stood heavily behind us. Louise looked up at him and said, "Oh, hello, Warren."

"Oh, hello, Warren," he simpered. "Am I interrupting anything? You go fishing together and you like to be in the dark together, and today you had a nice little nap together. Was it fun?"

She got up quickly. "What are you trying to say?"

"I'm telling you that you're a bitch. And I'm telling you I'm not stupid."

"You're just drunk, Warren," she said in a tired voice.

"Bitch," he said. "Stupid bitch."

"Watch it!" I said.

He swayed and peered at me. "Here comes noble white knight to the rescue. Galumph, galumph. After lunch and that tiring, tiring morning fishing you are both soooo tired. So you took naps. So I went back to the room, and what do you know, no sleepy little wife. Where could she be? I wonder. So I went tippytoe to the window of the room of the big young industrial genius and I couldn't see in, but I could hear real good. You two were having *such* a nice active nap. Did the tropics get to you, honey?"

"You don't know what you're saying, Warren. I couldn't sleep. I walked west along the beach, looking for shells. The shells I found are in a paper bag on my bureau."

"Bitch, bitch, bitch," he said with satisfaction. "I heard you, you bitch. Moaning and sighing. I heard you."

"You heard somebody else," I said. "Not Louise."

In the silence she gave a little gasp. I suspect that if she were shot through the heart, she might give the same little gasp before crumpling to the ground. She walked quickly away from us and she was running by the time she reached the end of the dock.

"You put on a good act, you filthy bastard," Warren said.

"Just get away from me. Get the hell away from me."

I never saw the punch. The side of my jaw blew up and, after a curious interlude of weightlessness, I landed flat on my back in the water below the dock. The water cleared my head. I am so big I have never had to do much fighting. People think it over a long time before taking the risk of starting anything. I have an amiable streak that makes me think that fighting a man with your fists is stupid.

But I was very, very tired of Warren Dodge and I was in a kind of ferment of despair over how he had forced me to ruin Louise's opinion of me.

I swam to where I could walk, and I walked ashore. He was waiting for me. I knew his reputation as an able and savage brawler. I am reasonably coordinated, but not fast. During my brief football career I depended on power rather than speed.

He waited for me up on the lawn and we circled cautiously in the shifting light. Then he yelled. I knew what he wanted. He wanted the others to come and watch how he could cut the bigger man down. It worked. They came out. Mike bulled his way between us and said, "You both think this is necessary?" We said it was. "So go ahead then."

He came in and hooked me three times on the jaw and once in the stomach and I clubbed him hard, but too high on the head. It hurt my hand. He came in again, and it was the same sort of thing, but I hit him a little bit better. I didn't think about the pain or the blood in my mouth or the people watching. I thought about staying on my feet and getting that one solid blow. The pattern was set. It was the only thing I could do.

"Fall . . . damn you. Fall!" he said, and I knew he was winded. It gave me a little hope, and hope made me just a little bit quicker. And when he came in again, I knocked him down. He got up quickly and tried again and I knocked him down. He got up slowly and I walked toward him but he didn't wait. He dropped down onto his knees and said, "Thass enough!"

"Apologize!" I said. My voice sounded thick and funny.

"Okay, okay. I'm sorry."

I walked by him and up to the house, marching on doughy legs. Amparo Blakely took over. She had a first aid kit in her room. She had done some nursing once upon a time. All the time she was fixing me up, her hands very gentle, she was saying, "How perfectly asinine! Grown men acting like naughty little boys. I've never seen anything so ridiculous in my life."

"Sometimes it's the only thing you can do."

"Nonsense! There! You're not half as bad as I thought you would be. Let me see that hand."

It was puffy and it hurt. She prodded my knuckles and made me work my fingers until she was reasonably certain I hadn't broken anything. I could wiggle one tooth with my tongue tip. There were lumps on my jaw and cuts inside my mouth, and the one he had landed on my throat had hoarsened my voice.

When we went out the fight was still being discussed. Warren had gone to his room without a word of explanation to anyone. I was handed a drink and then they demanded that I tell them what it was about.

"He was tight and nasty," I said. "I was sitting on the dock with Louise and we were talking business. He put a wrong interpretation on it. When I stood up he knocked me off the dock. I better go put some dry clothes on."

"Maybe you ought to go to bed," Amparo said.

"Not for a while. I don't feel too bad."

"You will," she said, meaningfully.

After I ceased being the center of attention, I found myself alone with Amparo. We sat on the veranda. She was a woman who could maintain a very comfortable and comforting silence.

"Mike says you're thinking about joining our clan," she said after a while.

"It needs consideration."

"I think you'd like it. It's . . . what do they call it? . . . a taut ship."

"Flying the jolly roger?"

"According to the opposition."

"How about according to you, Amparo?"

"Well . . . I wouldn't call it a pirate ship, but I wouldn't say we don't have our moments. I'd say privateer."

"You're just fiddling around with semantics, aren't you?"

"Maybe. But it's exciting. Of that you can be sure. Never a dull moment in Deanland."

"Have you been with him long?"

"For more years than I care to think about. Mike's anxious to have you aboard. There's some hot spots coming up where he can use you."

"Hasn't he got anybody else?"

"Sure. But Mike has the idea that you get better service from the able and hungry young men. How are you feeling now, Sam?"

"A little shaky."

She patted my arm. "You better go off to bed, really. And try to sleep in if you can."

SIX

When I woke up at the usual six-thirty on Friday morning, I felt like hell. Every joint and muscle ached and twanged when I climbed laboriously out of bed. A long hot shower eased some of the anguish. The mirror told me my puffed mouth was back almost to normal. The tooth didn't feel quite as loose. My right hand was damned sore. When I walked quietly down the veranda the bright morning had a garish look of unreality about it.

I felt that the place was changing me, and I wished I was back in my familiar office. Life moved a little too fast here, and it was a little too rotten ripe for my tastes. I thought about the papers waiting for my signature and I knew that the scene on the dock had, at least, done one thing. Until I knew which way Louise was going to jump, I had no decision to make. It could well be that any chance of further co-operation between us had been lost.

Booty came out to take my breakfast order while I was still wallowing in the pool. I clung to the side and gave her the order. Yesterday's burn showed fine promise of eventually turning into a tan. Booty brought my breakfast and then backed up and stood there. I looked at her and she had her underlip caught in white strong teeth and she looked shyly troubled.

"What is it, Booty?"

"You fight that mon. I hear you beat that mon."

"Yes, I guess I did."

"I am glad."

"Don't you like him?"

"I do not like that mon. No. When I am in a room

94

and I am cleaning, he wants me to do an evil thing. And that mon laughed when I run. I do not tell. I do not know if I should tell Mr. Dean."

I thought quickly. "No, Booty. Don't tell Mr. Dean. I'll speak to Mr. Dodge. He won't bother you again."

"Thank you very much, sar. But all the same I will have with me a knife. Here." She touched the side of her right thigh lightly, touched the white starch of her skirt. She turned and walked away.

I could think of very few men aside from Warren Dodge who would try anything like that.

At seven-thirty Louise came along in a different swim suit, a yellow one. She had a slightly sallow look and there were dark smudges under her eyes. She gave me a cool nod and one millimeter of formal smile, put her towel and lotion and dark glasses on the edge of the pool, tucked her dark hair into a white cap and dived in. I sipped my coffee and watched her sleek stroke. After she pulled herself out she headed for a far table.

"Sit here, Louise," I said.

She hesitated, came back and sat opposite me. "Thank you," she said. She made a small formal ceremony of sitting down. In the process she erected a glass wall between us, perfectly transparent and about three inches thick. We could converse through it by means of an electronic communication system.

"How is Warren?"

"The left side of his face looks horrible," she said, and I thought I saw a little gleam of satisfaction.

"We seem to be the earliest birds in the outfit."

"Yes, don't we?" Booty came out and Louise ordered toast and coffee.

I braced myself and said, "Any comment on that ugly little scene last night?"

She looked at me without change of expression. "Should I have?"

"Any general opinion then?"

"I decided in the night that Mr. Dean is perfectly

capable of representing my ownership interest and my brother's in Harrison."

"I see. When is he going to find out about this?"

"Just as soon as I see him. Then I am going to request transportation back to Grand Bahama."

"That's right. There'd be no point in staying on."

"Aren't you going to make some sort of violent protest?"

"Would it do any good?"

"No."

"Then why should I waste my time? I'd think you'd have a little more editorial comment to make, Louise."

There was a flash of anger. "Don't look so damn superior and tolerant. This is a cheap place full of cheap people. This place has a reek of sex and liquor and decay."

"And I'm as cheap as the rest of them?"

"You seem to fit in admirably. I know when Warren is lying and I know when he's bluffing, and I know when he's telling the truth."

"Let's back up a minute, Louise. Just to get a little perspective. What the hell does my *personal* life have to do with whether or not I can run the Harrison Corporation? And who are you to sit in judgment and condemn me?"

"Who said I was?"

"Oh, come off it." I paused while Booty brought her breakfast. When Booty was out of earshot I said, "I suppose I ought to be flattered."

"How do you mean?"

"That you should care so much about my habits."

"I care this much. I didn't think you were cheap or callous or so . . . uncontrolled. I respected you. While I respected you, I trusted you. Now I can no longer respect or trust you, and doesn't it follow that I can no longer think you're the man to run Harrison?"

"It might follow, in some kind of illogical female way, I suppose."

"But, Sam," she said with a pleading note in her voice. "You don't even *know* any of these women!"

"Have you been over the list? Now who could it have been? Amparo, Elda, Bridget, Lolly, Tessy, Bonny. All quite suitable, I'm sure."

"Don't be such a vile pig, Sam. How could I know? For all I know it was Booty, on a sort of room service basis."

"That was a foul thing to say, Louise. I suspect that Booty is a lady. More of a lady than most of the female guests. If you want to be assured that Booty is unattainable, check with your husband. She brushed him off."

"That's a damn lie!"

"Once again Louise, our gentle heroine, springs to the spirited defense of her utterly useless husband. It can get pretty tiresome, dear. Very monotonous. Maybe if you had some spunk you would have let me know you're in love with me."

She gasped and tried to sneer but her eyes filled with tears. She looked at me and her mouth trembled and she said, "I nearly was, Sam. I . . . very nearly was."

And she ran for the house. A woman is not at her best running away from you in a tight bathing suit. I tried to feel something tender and special toward her. I couldn't. I was too annoyed at being condemned without a trial. And disappointed at her crack about Booty. And a little distressed at a smallness of mind which let too much emotion overlap into a business deal. All I could think of was that she'd had a damn small breakfast. Three bites of toast, three sips of coffee. And she left her rubber cap, sun glasses, lotion and towel behind. I was sick of scenes and I was sick of slickness and maneuverings. And I was getting tired of the damn sunshine and the unspeakably glorious weather.

Bridget came out of the house and stopped and looked back in the direction where Louise had disappeared. She wore a light blue workshirt and she had her hands in the pockets of blue jean shorts. She came out to the table and looked at Louise's breakfast. She sat down at my right and said, "What's with her?"

"Off in what they call a huff."

"By the way, good morning. You don't seem marked up, ole Sam. I'll betcha Warren isn't pretty. I was standing there wringing my hands until my knuckles cracked, and every time you hit him I could feel it in the pit of my stomach."

"Today I feel very elderly."

"This is the first time we've been alone . . ." she paused and colored slightly ". . . since I made such a fool of myself. I expect I ought to feel all quivery and girlish and abject."

"Go right ahead."

"But I don't." She tilted her head to the side and seemed to study me. "I feel pretty darn comfortable with you. Almost as if you could understand, which I doubt."

"Why do you doubt it?"

"I am not precisely a female who stops the town clock when she goes to market. And I flang myself at you. And, being male, you will think I did it because of your overpowering charm."

"I think you did it because you felt lost and lonesome and helpless. I was a pair of arms to comfort you and a chest to cry on. And what it turned into wasn't anybody's fault."

"But I got up and went to the door and closed it. I could just as easily have walked right on out and I darn near did."

"Glad you didn't."

"I keep fighting that line of thought, brother. But so am I glad I didn't. So there. Let's drop the subject forever. And if that's a gleam in your eye, kindly remove it. There are no return engagements in this conference. But before we drop the subject, let me tell you one teensy little thing that has been accomplished. Last night, for a while, I hung over Guy's shoulder while he played poker. I was all full of giddy warmth and unrequited devotion. And suddenly things weren't *quite* the same."

"How?"

"I looked down and saw how carefully he'd arranged his poor hair so that it would cover the most of the bald spot and I wanted to pat his poor old bald head because it was kinda touching, and then I saw the place where he didn't quite get all her lipstick off. It was in that orange shade she uses, and suddenly I didn't want to pat his bald head any more. Nor did I want to bash it in with a club. But I hung around long enough to watch him stay on a pair of threes, and draw twice to an inside straight. I learned my poker from my daddy. Daddy could have cleaned poor Guy in one long session. So maybe a cure is beginning to take place, and maybe you have some part in it. And thanks. Now we drop the subject and we get onto Louise for a moment. Why did she flee by me, snuffling and blubbering?"

I told her. In detail. When I finished she put her hand on my wrist. "Oh, honestly, you poor guy! What a filthy break that was. There I go again, barging in on people and messing up their lives. Sam, I'm terribly sorry."

"The damage is done. Poetic justice or something. This place is loaded with voyeurs."

"What do you mean?"

I told her about Jack Buck, Lolly and Tessy Crown. She turned grayish under her tan and closed her eyes and said, "Gah!"

"That's a good word."

"Taking the top off Tessy's skull would be like lifting a damp rock. I don't condemn Lolly too much. She's spoiled rotten. She's a vicious bawdy little pushover. And you can't blame Jack Buck for taking what's available. But to have her own stepmother . . . I wish to hell you weren't so good at describing things,

Sam'l. That little scene is going to take a lot of forgetting. Look, honey, I'm going to have a little chat with Louise."

"If you mean what I think you mean, no."

"There's no possible way you can stop me. Call it penance. I'll bare my simple soul and my base instincts. I'll tell her how it happened. My God, if it hadn't happened after I started to chaw on your neck, you'd be considerably less than human, I suspect. Can you see yourself pushing me sternly away and giving me a lecture on self-restraint?"

"Hardly."

"Sam'l, darling, you were a sitting duck and I blasted your little white feathers all over the landscape. I can make Louise see that, I know. We'll have some girl talk."

"I'd rather you wouldn't."

"There's nothing you can do about it. What happened to Booty? I'm about to starve!"

"All right then. If I can't stop you, I'll do some high-level scheming along with everybody else. Try to get to her before she gets to Mike."

She looked puzzled for a moment and then said, "Oh, I get it. She's so hurt she wants to smash your little red wagon."

"And her own too, possibly."

"Seems a little bratty, doesn't it?"

"Maybe."

"So duty first. I can eat any time."

When she was halfway across the lawn toward the house she turned and took one hand out of her pocket and waved at me.

At a little after nine-thirty the *Try Again* set off with Mike and Amparo, Tommy and Puss aboard. I had not seen Louise or Bridget again. I saw them when I was out on the dock. They were way along the sand beach in the sunshine, walking together, a tiny figure in yellow and a tiny figure in blue. It made me feel very odd. I selected tackle from the

dock house and headed the other way, back toward
the rocks.

Skylark was not there, but the minnows were. I
took some gang hooks off a plug and rigged a way
to snatch them. I pulled one minnow out in about
every six tries, and too often he was mortally
wounded. I got a couple of meager barracuda, and
then a rather small yellowtail. I was about to throw
him back and then decided to try him as bait. He
was too big to cast, but he was most agreeable about
swimming straight out. I let him go as far as he
wanted to. After a little while there was a long hard
steady pull. I set the hook. It wasn't a barracuda. It
didn't jump. The line did not go out with any great
speed, but it went out with a fearful regularity. I
could have achieved the same effect by sinking the
hook into the transom of a cabin cruiser moving at
trolling speed. When I saw there was no stopping it
or turning it, I tightened the drag until the line
snapped. Fortunately it snapped out next to the
leader.

A needle fish took the next minnow and when it
leaped and skittered and threw minnow and hook,
a good barracuda took the minnow in the air, a few
inches above the water. Though not as big as
Louise's, it was a long fight. I beached him and released him, and as he was much fresher than Louise's,
he went on out very briskly.

It seemed enough for a time and I found a rock
flat enough to sit on. The fishing had been good, but
it was not like the day before. I had the ghost of
Louise with me, a laughing Louise, talking to the
great fish while Skylark and I watched her. And I
had other ghosts. White paper ghosts in the drawer
of a writing desk in Mike's room.

I tried to push it all out of my mind and be a
part of the empty rocky beach, and the sun and the
sky and the water. From where I sat I could see no
sign that man had ever existed on this planet. I

knew that after I was dead a thousand years, these rocks would look the same. An imperceptible half millimeter of surface would be worn away. Ten billion conchs would have died in the sun on the rocks. The incredibly remote descendants of the barracuda we had caught would be swimming out there, stalking their game.

There was a tide pool near my feet. I looked down into it and saw the black sea urchins, saw two unhurried questing minnows a half inch long. I had tossed a dead minnow into that pool not a half hour ago. It was almost invisible, almost entirely covered with small brown snails who seemed to be trying to shoulder each other out of position.

I thought of myself and I felt small and I wondered if I wasn't being pretty damn pretentious in sweating and fussing over moralities and ethics. How many shares of common stock can dance on the point of a needle?

I wasn't going to kill anybody. I wasn't going to wear a black mask and steal. I was for hire in the market place, and Mike Dean had made the best offer.

I was a part of the vast cycle of life and death, and this was my one turn around the track, so I'd better run as gaudy a race as possible.

I got up and tried again, using a plug this time. I foul-hooked a horrible looking thing of about eight pounds. He put up a frenzied but lethargic and wallowing battle. He was black and he was mostly head and he had black spines all over him. He had two huge blue eyes. He had plates of bone in his mouth rather than teeth. When I got a stick to pry his mouth open, he bit it off. I worked the plug loose with my knife blade. When I rolled him into the water with my foot, he showed his gratitude by putting one of his spikes through my canvas shoe and into my toe.

I got back to the house a little after noon. I met Warren on the veranda as I was heading for my room. He tried to go right on by but I stopped him. I was shocked at the damage I had done. Shocked and, I must admit, pleased. The left side of his face, from hairline to jaw, was puffed out and empurpled. His left eye was swollen entirely shut.

He stood with my hand on his arm and he looked flatly at the center of my chest and said, "What do you want?"

I kept my voice down. "No more games with Booty. You understand?"

"You're all through at Harrison, Glidden. You're finished there."

"Are you too tight to understand what I mean about Booty?"

"I understand you all right."

"Well?"

"Okay, okay. No more games. What do you want me to say?"

I let go of his arm. I watched him walk away.

I had lunch with Guy Brainerd, Elda Garry and Cam Duncan. Elda was being very elfin. Guy was loaded with heavy-handed courtliness. I went to my room after lunch. I stretched out on the bed again. I had a plaintive wish for Bridget to stop by again, and I pushed it out of my mind and was soon asleep.

Someone shook my shoulder gently. I opened my eyes. Louise was beside the bed, sitting on her heels, her face a foot from mine. In the dim light that came into the room her expression was very tender and loving.

"Are you awake, Sam?"

"I am now." I propped myself up on my elbow and reached for my cigarettes. She accepted one. She sat rather timidly on the edge of the bed, a safe distance away.

"I'm sorry about the way I acted."

"Bridget talked to you. I didn't want her to."

"She's terribly coarse, darling, but there's some-

thing nice about her, I think. Some essential honesty.
She made me understand . . . how and why it happened. So I had to come and apologize."

"You didn't have to."

"Please, Sam. Don't be gruff. I want to forgive you
if you'll let me."

"Let me get this straight. You want to forgive me."

"Of course. You know, you were very naughty."

"I was a very, very naughty man," I said, remembering the tweak that Cam had bestowed on Elda.

"Of course you were. But we shouldn't start with
a misunderstanding."

"Start?"

"I'm through defending him, Sam. I'm through
being stupid and loyal to someone who isn't worth
it. I'm going to get a divorce."

"Does he know that?"

"Not yet. But he soon will, believe me."

"And then we get married."

"Yes, darling. It's perfect. It should have happened
long ago. We've lost so much precious time. When
you kissed me out there on the dock I knew."

"So now what do you tell Mike Dean?"

"Sam, you're acting so . . . odd. I know I hurt you.
And I know you do feel a little guilty. Darling, how
can I prove to you it has all come true?"

"I don't know."

She looked at me and looked away. She said, very
delicately, "Warren is out by the pool, out like a
light." She was wearing black shorts and a green
sleeveless blouse. She toyed with the buckle on the
shorts. She seemed to heave some sort of inward
sigh and said with modesty and a kind of regret and
a certain tinge of martyrdom, "If you really want
me to, darling. If it would mean a great deal to you
to . . . love me now."

"I wouldn't want you to sacrifice yourself, Louise."

"I think it would be so much better if we waited,
actually." She made a little face. "I wouldn't be able

to forget that . . . this is where it happened with her. It would spoil it for me."

"But a big coarse brutal guilty male wouldn't be bothered by all those little nuances."

"You keep sounding so odd."

"I'm an odd guy."

"But I'm going to get used to you. You can at least kiss me."

She felt good under my hands and I guess her response was all that could be desired. Her lips were moist and parted and she breathed hard. And then she wriggled free as though I were about to be naughty, and put her mouth close to my ear and whispered that she loved me. And then she went out, smiling back at me.

Boy wins girl. Boy wins rich girl. High school dream comes true at last.

But I wished to God she wouldn't remind me so strongly of a brunette Elda Garry. And I wished I didn't have the horrible suspicion that that smoldering look was misleading.

I couldn't go back to sleep.

When I heard the *Try Again* coming in, I looked at my watch and found it was only a little after three. I pulled on my clothes and went down to the dock.

SEVEN

THE FISHERMEN were full of high spirits, pleased with each other and the boat and the day. They had brought two sail and a marlin to gaff and released them. Puss had hung the marlin and both Tommy and Mike said she had performed like an expert. She had reel blisters and aching shoulders.

They brought back a renewed spirit of holiday that affected the rest of the group. Calypso records were piled on the changer. Everybody congregated at the pool.

As soon as I had changed I intercepted Mike when he was away from the others and said, "I'll sign up, Mike."

"Good! Good!" he said heartily, but I could have sworn that for a moment there was a slight look or expression of disappointment.

"When do I sign?"

"No hurry about the details. Just one fast question, Sam. Will I get the proxies?"

"You will now."

He nodded. He wasn't using any charm on me. There was no handshake of welcome to the club, glad you're aboard. I was one of Mike Dean's boys now, and by God, I was going to be used. I hoped I'd be used so extensively I wouldn't have very much time to think about all the things that might have been. I would ride the crest until I had it made, and then I would bow out and buy into a little business of my own. A nice clean little business. And be productive and constructive as hell.

And right now I could start celebrating. Tomorrow

everybody would be signing papers. And maybe tomorrow we would be leaving. I wondered just how
the hell I would go about explaining it all to Cary
and Gene and Al and Walt. They would think I'd
been had. They'd think I'd sold out. I knew I hadn't
been had. I knew I hadn't sold out. I was playing it
just the way any one of them would have played it
had they been given the same opportunity.

What was going to happen wasn't my fault. It was
Tom McGann's. They could blame the dead.

Time to celebrate.

So, for the second time in my life, I got royally
and ponderously drunk. I am big and so it takes a
lot. I took a lot. I don't remember dinner. I was celebrating. Mike Dean's new boy. Hooray. One third of
a millionaire. And my old man never made more than
fifty-five bucks a week in his life.

The afternoon swirled around me and plunged
into the night. After a session of complete blackouts
and partial blackouts, memory is sadly fragmented.
I think I did a lot of dancing, and I can remember
trying to play pingpong, and I can remember adding
an uncertain basso profundo to some barbershop
singing. And I can remember a time of dubious clar-
ity when I sat out on the dock with Bonny Carson
and we had a bottle which we handed back and
forth at stately intervals. I was explaining to her about
the cycle of life and death and your one turn around
the track and how just about any human activity you
can think of is pretty damn meaningless. She was
telling me in between times how meaningless her
life was. Every time either of us would say anything beautiful, we'd get tears in our eyes and we'd
kiss each other tenderly and moistly and then pass
the bottle again.

I woke up at six-thirty. I was on top of the bed.
I wasn't undressed. Half my brain was broken glass
and the other half was rusty rivets. They clattered

together when I moved. I plodded into the bathroom. I was thoroughly pasted with lipstick and there was an inexplicable scratch on my chin. I had the queasy trembles and the black remorses.

A half hour later, feeling but slightly better, I was sitting at the pool over a second cup of black coffee and wondering whether I could risk any kind of food when Bridget Hallowell appeared, disgustingly bright and cheerful. She wore a little blue and white checked sun suit, very brief. Her legs were long and golden and very lovely.

I covered my eyes with my hands and looked out at her through a little space between two fingers.

"The life of the party," she said.

"Don't."

"Oh, the things you said. And the things you *did!*"

"My God, Bridget."

She laughed. "All right, ole Sam'l. I've got a kind heart. I'll take you off the hook. You neither said nor did anything disgraceful. You were just a big happy smiling drunk, harmless and childlike in your beautiful simplicity. You kissed all the women and you kept shaking hands with everybody."

"How did I get to bed?"

"Bonny came in crying. She said you were dead. She said you were full of beautiful thoughts, but you were dead. She wanted somebody to get a shovel because she was going to bury you personally right where you had fallen. We inspected the body. Fletcher and Cam lugged it back to the room and came back dusting their hands and looking superior. Look around and see if you notice anything missing."

It took longer than it should have before I saw that the *Portess* was gone.

"They left at daybreak," she said. "Your amiable little debauch will be completely overlooked in view of what happened later. That was really juicy. Are you in so much pain you can't hear me?"

"I can hear you."

"Jack Buck had been sweet-talking Puss McGann. I guess he thought it was time. So he maneuvered her into the night. She fought him until I guess she realized that he was very, very determined. So she had sense enough to scream. And, very fortunately, she was heard. I had a good ringside seat to your little go-round with Warren, and I had just as good a seat at this one, but this one was no contest. That cute little Tommy gave away four inches and thirty pounds. But he moved so fast you could hardly see him. I don't think Jack Buck landed punch one. It didn't take a minute and a half for Tommy to cut him to ribbons and knock him colder than a press agent's heart. Mike got indignant and told Port Crown he ought to fire Buck. Port got up on his horse and told Mike it was none of his damn business. Mike told Port that he was willing to admit Texas has the biggest of everything. They've got people with more money and less sense than any other state in the union. Port told Mike that he'd yank the rug out from under him in their Crown-Dean Corporation. Mike said to go ahead and be damned and kindly get himself and his funny looking boat and his round-heeled daughter and his hunky wife off the island just as damn well soon as he could, and if he wanted to leave Jack Buck behind, they'd cut strip bait off him and troll with it tomorrow and see if they could find any catfish with strong stomachs. Port told Mike to come to Texas and he'd shoot him dead. And stumped off to bed. So, darling Sam, nobody is going to remember that you were a little squiffed. You've been upstaged."

"I am grateful."

"I see that you are patched up with Louise."

"Thanks to you."

"She was pretty tough to talk to. She had a hard time understanding my motives. Are you certain you can get all your messages across?"

"I don't know."

"It's worth a try. She's a very handsome dish. I'd trade all my talent for a chance to look like that."

"You look just fine."

"Oh, thank you, sir, thank you, sir."

"What are your plans for the day?"

"That's up to dear Elda. She has the vivid and entertaining article I wrote." She went into a startlingly effective imitation of Elda Garry. "It's so perfectly charming, darling, so terribly valid and significant, but don't you think it may be just a fraction too frivolous? We, at *Blend*, are doing a sincere job of putting out a valid book for young Americans. And, after all, aren't we dealing with very real and serious matters here?"

"Like that?"

"And then I'll rewrite three or four times for dear old Elda, and then she'll stick some real wet Eldaisms into my copy before it's printed up, and then all those young Americans will get a real and valid and significant puff job about Mike Dean, American. That's how it's done, sweetie. That's how the wheels go round."

She looked toward the house and said, "And now, being terribly sensitive and tactful and so on, I shall flee. Because here comes the Lady of Shalott." She left the table. Louise joined me. She was back in the pink swim suit with the black trim. She managed to look radiant and tremulous and faintly disapproving, all at the same time.

"Good morning, my darling," she said. "Wasn't that girl sitting with you? And how is your poor head?"

"The head thumps. And Bridget was sitting with me. She briefed me on what happened after I folded."

"It was horrible, really. Mike was awfully angry. I'm glad they're gone. They were unwholesome people. But I really don't see why there has to be so much fighting all the time. Honey, why did you drink so much?"

"Well, I guess I was sort of celebrating."

She patted my hand. "I was so afraid you'd go around saying why you were celebrating. I mean it would have been embarrassing for me, don't you see? I've got to tell Warren in my own time in my own way, and I don't want one of these hasty things. They're in such bad taste, don't you think? I think there should be some time between a divorce and another marriage. And I certainly won't be seen in public with you until the divorce is final. You do understand, don't you?"

"Yes, I understand." If, out of ten thousand shares you can clear a third of a million, add on her fifty thousand shares and you can sit back on cloud eighty with two million bucks. Maybe less than that, though, because it might be smart to start dumping it ahead of Mike's target quotation of fifty-four.

"I talked to Mike and Cam last night. Amparo is going to have the papers ready for Tommy and me to sign this morning. Then tomorrow, Sunday, we'll go over to Grand Bahama in the morning and Mike's plane will be waiting. Guy and Elda and that girl will go with us."

"Her name is Bridget."

"I know, darling. You don't have to be so fierce and protective about her. I told you that I'm willing to forget it ever happened. Anyway, we'll be flying from West Palm Beach to New York to leave them off, and we'll be home by five or six o'clock tomorrow night."

"There's just one little loose end, Louise. This business of the proxies. You decided to go ahead."

She gave me a round-eyed look. "But darling! Don't you remember? Oh, good morning, Booty. Toast and hot tea, please."

"And some more coffee, please," I said.

"Darling, last night you took Tommy and me out

on the veranda and you told us that you'd changed your mind, and you felt it would be a wonderful opportunity for the Harrison Corporation for Mike Dean to take control. You said you'd been mistaken about him."

Another blackout. In a sense it made it easier. It was something I had wondered about. I had wondered if, when the chips were down, I could force myself to look Louise and Tommy in the eye and tell them to go ahead. And I wondered if subconsciously I had willed myself to get drunk in order to get over that particular hurdle.

And I suddenly heard myself talking glibly, talking myself out of another hole, out of another awkward situation. "I was mistaken about him, Louise. I want you to do me a favor. When I get back I've got to keep on working with Dolson and the boys. And I'm afraid they might misinterpret my change of heart. So it will be easier on me if we let them believe that you signed your vote over to Mike in spite of my objections."

She looked puzzled, but said, "If you say so, darling."

That made it nice and easy. I could be buddy-buddy with the boys right up until June second when the papers I would sign would take effect. And then it wouldn't matter. I would be officially one of Mike Dean's boys and I wouldn't have to explain a damn thing to them. Why should I owe them an explanation anyway? Any one of them would have jumped at the chance. Boy, I was turning into a real sharp operator.

I'd be a credit to the organization. An ace up every sleeve. And, of course, the reason I felt like vomiting was because of the hangover.

After breakfast, after Louise swam and then stretched her flawless and lovely body out in the morning sun, I wandered away and went to Mike's room. I could hear voices inside. I knocked and somebody said to come in.

Mike and Bowman and Cam and Amparo were there. Amparo was taking stenographic notes. They smiled at me, but I sensed a faint annoyance at the interruption.

"Sorry to butt in. Louise and Tommy will sign the proxies this morning."

"It's all set," Mike said, "and everything is ready and I'm glad you were able to work it out with them."

"One other thing. I'd appreciate it if my . . . other arrangements with you weren't mentioned to them." I saw Cam give Amparo a glance of wry amusement and I felt my face get hot.

"We had no intention of mentioning it, Sam," Mike said. "As far as anybody outside this room knows or will know, we arrived at our agreements on the second day of June, the day after the Board of Directors met for the purpose of electing directors and appointing the officers of the Harrison Corporation. And so long as you're here, there's no reason why you shouldn't sign right now."

It didn't take long. There was a little business of witnesses, and a little business with Amparo's notary seal.

I said, "According to the way this one is notarized, I signed it in New York City."

"On June second you will be in New York City," Bowman said.

"Oh. Well . . . excuse the interruption."

They started talking again before I had the door completely shut. I heard Cam say, "Wire Charlie to cease all drilling oper . . ."

I had the feeling that with Harrison in the bag, they were off at a gallop after other game. I had the feeling I was looming a hell of a lot smaller on the Dean horizon. I went out onto the veranda. Little Bundy was there. He cornered me. I couldn't miss

if I'd put a little money into "*Say It Again,*" starring
Bonny Carson. It was going to be big. It was going
to be the biggest ever. Bonny was singing better than
ever. She'd knock them in the aisles. And good old
Mike had practically promised to put a heavy piece
of money in the show. The choreography would knock
them dead. Take like, for example, the second act
curtain, where . . .

"Hold it a minute," I said.

"You decided to come in?" he asked, his face all
lighted up.

"I didn't decide that. I decided Bonny is a lush. I
decided she's lost her voice and her timing. I decided that maybe Mike has got you two down here
for comedy relief. I decided I wouldn't walk across
the street to see your big show that'll never happen
if they paid the customers ten dollars to sit through
it."

And I left him standing there. Two minutes later I
was so damned ashamed of myself I wished I could
drop dead on the spot. I tried to tell myself that I'd
never been the type to pull the wings off flies. It
wasn't like me to be vicious and brutal without
cause.

And a few moments later I knew why I had done
it. I was ashamed of myself because Mike Dean had
maneuvered me through my own greed. I was
ashamed of the way I was going to be kicking some
pretty nice people in the face. So I had to pull ridiculous little Bundy down to my level. I had to spit
on his dreams.

I went back but he was gone. I don't know what I
could have said, or whether it would have done any
good. Tommy was down on the dock, sitting crosslegged and working on a spear gun. I went down
there because it was somebody to talk to and because I felt uncomfortable being alone.

"The winnah, in one minute and twenty seconds
of the first round . . ."

He looked up and grinned at me. "Damn good thing that boy was muscle-bound." He stopped grinning. "Puss is so damn naïve sometimes. She thinks everybody in the world is just dandy. And she's so friendly that punks like that Jack Buck can get the wrong idea. He certainly scared hell out of her. He had her stripped to the waist, and it was a lucky thing Bowman heard her yell."

"This Dubloon Cay seems to bring out the best in everybody," I said.

He put the spear gun aside and lighted a cigarette. "It's been reminding me of something and I couldn't think of what it was, and last night I remembered. It's a hell of a lot like the wartime deal. I mean it has that same flavor. Like in London. People drinking too much and brawling and concentrating on sex as though it was the last chance they'd ever have. Maybe it's a funny kind of a tension. Or just being on an island. It's as if we tossed the rules overboard."

It was the first time I had ever heard any kind of serious talk from Tommy McGann.

"Maybe the tension comes from people trying to make decisions."

"I understand my sainted sister has arrived at a decision. About Warren. And she's elected you."

"Do you object?"

"No, I don't object. Hell, you know Warren. I can get along with him when nobody else can. And I don't want to sound disloyal to Louise, but . . . Oh, the hell with it." He picked up the spear gun.

"Wait a minute. I want to know what you think."

He sighed and put the gun aside again. "First I have to explain about me. I spent a lot of years learning not to give a damn. Our father was a technically honest and emotionally dishonest man. He was that funny kind of hypocrite who can't admit for one split second that he ever did a wrong thing, ever made any kind of a mistake. And that made him an overbearing, emotionally crippling son of a bitch. It was like trying to live with a righteous avalanche. There just wasn't room in the house for anybody else's emotions or ideas. I reacted by not giving a damn. I guess by the time I was fifteen, the habit was set. Maybe it made me a good fighter pilot. Anyway, if I didn't give a damn, there wasn't any way he could hurt me. Without the money, I'd probably be a bum. But I inherited money and I married money. So I can play and I like to play, and so does Puss and it's a nice pleasant grasshopper life and I don't feel the least bit guilty about it. Now take Louise. She went the other way. She decided to suffer. You can feed on your own suffering, you know. And it becomes just as necessary after a while as the air you breathe. She's lived with a tragic picture of herself for a long time. And when she got married, which surprised me that she would, she married another peck of trouble. Warren makes her miserable. But that's just exactly what she has to have. If Warren tried in every way to make her happy, it still wouldn't work, because then she'd have to invent reasons for suffering. In a funny kind of way, it's a good marriage. I'm not trying to make her out as some kind of a monster. Our father was the monster. But it's something you should understand about her. And, if you understand it, maybe you can help her get over it. Maybe you could do it. I wish you all kinds of luck, and I know I've talked too damn much."

"I think I see what you mean."

"Don't let it put you off."

I saw movement out of the corner of my eye and looked toward the house. Louise came down across the lawn. "Tommy, they want us to come sign those proxies now."

"Okay," he said and stood up.

"You're sure you understand this is the best thing to do, like Sam says?" she asked him.

"Sign, schmine," he said. "A signature you want,

a signature you get. I don't bother my furry little head with the details, sis. All I want to do is get the spear gun fixed."

"Tommy, do you have to be so . . . trivial about everything?"

"I'm a trivial-type guy."

I stood and watched them go up across the graded lawn toward the main house, side by side. I had a feeling that something was slipping away from me. I wanted to go roaring after them and say, "It's all a big mistake, kids. Honest Sam Glidden is giving you and your children, if any, and your children's children a classic financial raping. And I get a big payoff. But maybe the only payoff will be in money because all of a sudden little sister doesn't look quite so good to me. So don't sign."

But of course I stood there and watched them out of sight, thinking of how strongly they resembled each other on the surface and how different they were down underneath where it counted.

Then I went back to my room to get more cigarettes. Bridget and Elda Garry and Guy Brainerd were having a conference on the veranda over a typed manuscript. Bridget winked at me without changing the bright-little-girl-in-school expression she was wearing. I liked the roundness of her face and the way her nose was slightly up-tilted. They were in shadow, but her hair looked as though a shaft of the sunlight had found its way down through the veranda roof.

When I came out of my room I met Warren Dodge just coming out of his. His face was improving slightly. The swelling had gone down and his eye was open, though not far, but he wore interesting shades of saffron, blue and purple.

"Welcome to the club," he said.

"How do you mean?"

"You look like hell. I never expected you to tie one on. I thought all you business wheels kept your guard up night and day. So you wouldn't spill any trade secrets. Maybe, for Chrissake, you're human. Anyhow, you've got one daisy of a right hand on you. Like being slapped with a cinder block. It was the first time in my life, compadre, that I didn't get back on my feet when I could have. I didn't happen to see any particularly bright future in it."

We walked along together. I said, "I don't know what was holding me up."

"Neither do I. I tagged you good. Let's find John and get a drink made. How does a rum sour sound?"

"Fine, if it'll stay down."

We found John and he brought ice and made us a drink at the playroom bar.

"Who was it in your room Thursday afternoon, pal?" he asked.

"No comment."

"I vote for Murphy. Process of elimination. That's a very choice bit, Glidden. When the Crowns took off, it screwed up a campaign I was working on. I would have hit pay dirt today. Not the kid. Tessy. So with that dream broken, I think I'll switch my sights to Murphy. Any objection?"

I was unprepared for anger that was like a half-blinding sheet of flame. "Stay the hell away from her!"

He grinned at me. "I wasn't sure it was her. So I ran a little check. Thanks for the information. John, this one was a little too sweet."

I left him there. I went to the pool. I swam ten lengths of the pool before my anger was entirely gone. When I climbed out I discovered I had forgotten to take the cigarettes and matches out of the waistband of my swim trunks. After I got a fresh pack from my room, I saw that Tommy was out beyond the end of the dock in fins, face mask and snorkel. Louise and Puss were sitting on the dock watching him. He did a surface dive and disap-

peared. He seemed to be gone for a long time. He
came up just as I reached the dock. He swam over
and clung to the stern of one of the skiffs, breathing hard.

"Pretty good hole out there," he said. "Lot of stuff
in it."

"Please be careful, honey," Puss said. She seemed
very subdued.

A few minutes later Warren came down to watch,
and so did Cam Duncan and Amparo Blakely. The
five of us sat in a row on the edge of the dock.

After a few more tries, Tommy swam over to the
dock and looked up at us and said, "I'm getting
pooped. Anybody want to try? How about you,
Sam?"

"I've never done it."

"Nothing to it. I can adjust the fins and mask to
fit you. And it's damn beautiful down there. Clearest
water I ever saw."

I gave him a hand and helped him up.

"There's about six big 'cuda hanging around, but
they won't bother you. They're just curious."

I stared at him and said, "Are you kidding?"

"No, I'm not kidding. Hell, I've been in with them
before, off the Florida Keys."

I thought of the head of the yellowtail and I said,
"Tommy, I wouldn't go down there with those things
for ten thousand dollars."

"Chicken!" Warren said harshly.

EIGHT

VIOLENCE GIVES NO WARNING, usually. But sometimes there is a curious forewarning. The world changes in a strange way. It can happen at an automobile race, or a bullfight, or at an air show—anywhere where death is an acknowledged participant.

One moment everything will be going well, the cars roaring nimbly into the turns, the *torero* fixing the bull for the kill, the airplane circling high, ready to release the parachutist.

And then the world will change. Colors will seem more vivid, outlines and shapes more precise, and there will be an odd feeling of hush. And soon, then, you know it will happen. The careening car will slam the wall to send the rag doll driver flopping high, pinned for one endless moment against the blue of the sky. The bull will swerve and when the horns come up they will thud deep into blood and tissue and bone, and the *torero*, carried high and jolting ludicrously, will ride his life out on the white horns and the hump of throwing muscle. The tiny figure will come endlessly down through the holiday sky from the circling plane, the tangled white of the chute as straight as the tail of a comet, and it will strike the baked August earth and rebound horridly to the height of a tall man. And the crowd noise is always the same, a grating concerted shriek that dies into a long gasping sigh.

"Chicken!" he said, and I looked along the dock at his bloated face with its look of contempt and hatred. And I felt the familiar hush that precedes violence.

"Don't be childish," I said as casually as I could.

"I just don't have any warm and kindly feelings toward barracuda. Frankly, they scare hell out of me."

He stood up. "Chicken bastard," he said. "Give me the stuff, Tommy."

Puss's short laugh had a brittle sound. Louise said, "Honey, Tommy's very good at it and you've only done it three or four . . ."

"Shut up," he said.

"She could be right," Cam Duncan said.

Warren was fixing the mask strap and Tommy, on his knees, was adjusting the heel straps of the fins. "You will shut up too," Warren said harshly. There seemed to be a driving urgency about him. I knew it was related to everyone having seen him refuse to get up the night we fought.

He jumped off the dock, spat into the mask, rinsed it out and adjusted it. Tommy leaned down and handed him the spear gun. "Don't be stupid enough to try for a 'cuda, boy," Tommy said.

"I'm not crazy," Warren said. He swam out from the dock, swam to where Tommy had been diving.

"Wait a minute!" Tommy called. "If you spear something, don't . . ." But Warren was gone. Tommy looked nervous and uncertain. He said, in a flat voice, "I was going to tell him that if he speared anything, not to haul it in. The 'cuda might try to hit it when he's taking it off the spear. But he's not likely to get anything. And maybe he knows enough not to do that anyway."

I hadn't seen the others get up, but we were all standing. With the angle of the sun and the wind riffles on the water, we could not see below the surface. And the world was very still.

He broke through the surface, head craned back, cords in his throat standing out. And he broke the silence with a monstrous bray of pain and outrage and terror. And the water around him was a red stain.

Tommy hit the water first in a flat racing dive. I saw Puss poise herself to dive in and I pulled her back and dived from where she had been standing. I heard Warren yell again, and this time it seemed to me there was less body to the yell. Tommy reached him before I did and had started to tow him toward shore, pulling him along by one wrist, kicking strongly. The red spread thickly in the water. For a few seconds I could not figure how to help without getting in the way. Then I swam behind Warren, ending each stroke with a firm push against him. When we reached shallow enough water, I picked him up and carried him to the low sea wall and laid him on the grass. Tommy ripped the mask off. Warren was whining weakly, his eyes squeezed shut, rolling his head from side to side.

"Hit him twice," Tommy said.

"Tourniquets, quick!" Amparo Blakely said in a voice of command. Puss was vomiting into the grass a dozen feet away. Cam jumped down into a skiff and he had a pocket knife out and was cutting lengths of nylon mooring line. I ran to the dock house, vaguely aware that people were pouring out of the house and hurrying down across the lawn. I snatched an unrigged glass boat rod and snapped it across my thigh, and snapped it again, and ran back with two pieces.

"The arm first," Amparo said. He had been hit on the under side of the right upper arm, close to the armpit. Half the biceps muscle was gone. Amparo was groping for the artery with her fingers, but the blood continued to pulse strongly with each beat of his heart. He had lost consciousness. Cam slipped the nylon loop over the inert and ruined arm and I inserted the piece of glass rod. I twisted it quickly as Amparo tried to work the loop into proper position. But it was slippery work, and the great bite had been taken so close to the armpit that there was very little room.

The jetting pulse of blood slowed and seemed to stop. Amparo sat back on her heels, her face gray, her bloodied hands resting carelessly on the thighs of her ruined skirt.

"Does that stop it?" I asked. She shook her head and I saw that I had misunderstood. I looked at his face. I released the improvised tourniquet and stood up. The other wound had stopped bleeding too. It was on the outside of his right thigh, slightly toward the back, and up near the buttock. It was badly shredded, and wide enough and deep enough to hold a grapefruit.

Warren did not look big any more. He looked grayish and quite shrunken and very old. The green swim fins were the final touch of ludicrous horror. Nobody had to ask if he was dead. It was far too obvious that his life had run quickly into the roots of the green lawn.

I saw Skylark standing beyond all the others, eyes wide and white, and I could see his lips soundlessly forming the word barracuda over and over. Mike Dean looked as if he had bitten into something very sour. Tommy was slowly pounding his fist into his palm and there was no expression on his face. Bowman wore a strange expression. He stood with his head tilted a little, and he looked puzzled, as though he heard some distant sound he couldn't identify. I wondered if he was acquiring his first true awareness of his own mortality. Bonny Carson stood spreadlegged, three fingers in her mouth, looking like a soiled, elderly, frightened child. Guy Brainerd's face expressed sincere and dignified disapproval of the entire incident. Elda Garry stood beside him, hugging his arm, her face against his shoulder. Bridget stood with her eyes shut, swaying. And I saw her lower herself to the grass in a gingerly way in a half faint.

And then I looked at Louise. She stood not far away, leaning forward from the waist, stood in a strangely tense way. From her expression she seemed not so much to be looking at him as inward at herself in a hypnoidal trance. And on her face was a revealing and sickening expression of exaltation. It was as though, of all the girls in her class, she had been selected to play Joan of Arc.

"For God's sake, cover him up!" Bundy squealed, breaking the spell that was over all of us. Cam went quickly and quietly to the dock house and came back with a paint-stained tarp and spread it over the body. Louise flung herself onto the tarp, sobbing in a lost and hysterical way, and everybody, it seemed, tried to ask questions at once.

"How did it happen?"

But only Warren knew how it had happened.

Tommy, later on, after he had dived and retrieved the spear gun and found that it had been fired, and found a fragment of fish flesh adhering to the barb that hadn't been there before, made a logical reconstruction of what had probably happened.

"He nailed a fish. God knows what it was. Then he should have come up and got out of the water and hauled the spear line up and hoped no barracuda would nail the struggling fish. But he wanted to show off. So he pulled the spear toward him. The blood in the water and the flapping fish got the barracuda all heated up, and they flashed in. I'd guess that one nailed the fish and the next one hit him in the leg. Then when he threw his arms up to head for the surface, another one hit at the white underside of his arm, because it may have looked something like a fish. It's a damn sorry way to die and the only good thing you can say about it is it didn't last very long."

As with all emergencies, it had to be handled by the conference method. Mike, Bowman, Amparo, Cam and Guy went into conference, and in a half hour they had all the answers. Bowman had contacted Nassau and had gotten in touch with the proper officials. A man who could issue the necessary certification of accidental death would fly up from Nassau to West End to inspect the body and talk to the witnesses. He had also made contact with the mainland, and Mike's plane would be at West End. The body would be flown to

West Palm Beach and turned over at once to a funeral director who would arrange for proper shipment north.

These decisions were given to us in a meeting of all hands aboard, with Fletcher Bowman acting as spokesman, and Mike Dean not present.

"Cam will accompany you people," Bowman said, "and you can be certain he'll see that everything is handled as quietly as possible."

"What do you mean, quietly?" Bridget asked.

"It isn't something we want to beat any drums about, is it? Death by barracuda is extremely rare. Maybe, Guy, you can enlighten . . . your employee."

Guy smiled at Bridget, a wise and tolerant smile. "Murphy, dear, I explained to Mike that this isn't the sort of publicity that helps anyone concerned, or helps the area. We *certainly* don't want any tabloid headlines saying 'Guest of Mike Dean Eaten by Barracuda.' I'm sorry, Mrs. Dodge. Perhaps that example was distasteful to you. I'm certain that it can be handled in such a way that it will be reported in the press that Mr. Dodge drowned. Knowing Cam as I do, I can safely say that he'll be able to convince all officials concerned of the wisdom of the decision."

"But that isn't what happened!" Louise said in a small voice. She looked, and sounded, both hurt and disappointed.

Guy Brainerd's answer showed he had more perception than I had given him credit for. "It doesn't have to be a deep dark secret, Mrs. Dodge. After a few days have passed, so the information would no longer be considered newsworthy, I'm sure you can tell your intimate friends, in confidence of course, just what did happen to your husband."

She sat back with a frail brave smile.

I was grimly amused at how quickly the first name rule was beginning to break up. Maybe a sudden and nasty death had made us all aware that we were strangers to one another.

"When do we go?" Tommy asked.

"Right after lunch. I believe you'll have time to pack before lunch. You and your wife and Mrs. Dodge and Cam."

"Aren't I a part of that group?" I asked.

Cam answered for Bowman. "I suggested that it would be easier and probably go more smoothly if it's just the members of the family, Sam. Then, when I release the news to the press in West Palm Beach this afternoon, I have a more legitimate reason to handle all press interviews myself. While I'm at the West End Airport this afternoon, I'll make reservations with Mackay Airlines for you and Guy and Miss Hallowell and Miss Garry to West Palm tomorrow, and while I'm in West Palm today I'll see what I can do about reservations north by commercial airline for you."

"Bonny and me want to get off this island too," Bundy said with unexpected belligerence.

Bowman looked at him calmly. "I'm certain Cam will be glad to make similar arrangements."

"Right," Cam said. "But you ought to remember, Bundy, we've got some oil people coming in next week."

"The hell with them," Bundy said. "I'd rather scrabble around for angels in the city. We're not doing any good here. It's May already and we haven't even got a house lined up."

Louise and I said our tender farewells on a settee on the veranda not far from my room door. She wore a dark dress and had managed to acquire the look of a woman in mourning for a dearly beloved husband.

"I have thanked God a hundred times that I didn't tell him I wanted a divorce. Then I would have had to blame myself."

"Very lucky," I said.

She took my hand in both of hers and held it.

"You're a sweet guy, Sam. But it must have been madness."

"You mean we could never have found happiness."

"That's right, my darling," she said, tears standing in her beautiful eyes, her perfect features like ancient ivory.

Tommy had clued me, and I had read the rest of it in her face when she had looked at her dead husband. She had to hurt. She had to be martyred. She fed on unhappiness. And now she would give me up gladly because she had the juiciest role of her life. She would soon come to believe that hers had been a perfect marriage. She would edit her memories until Warren lost all the whisky bloat, until he had never looked at another woman. And then she would be a darkly tragic figure with a story in which there was a delicious touch of the macabre. In the prime of his life, in the fullness of their love, her darling husband had been killed by barracuda. Or would it become sharks in time? And she could drift through the old house, and nurse her tragedy in her walled garden, and be deliciously miserable all the days of her life.

I was tempted to tell her just what she was doing, but I remembered the look in Bundy's eyes as I had turned away from him after speaking my little piece. If she wanted to hoke it up, the least I could do was play along.

So I lifted her hand to my lips and kissed it and said, "I'll spend the rest of my life thinking of what might have been." I did not mention the intense relief I would feel whenever I would think of it.

"You're a dear, Sam. I'll see you back home, of course, but we will be very correct with each other, won't we?"

"No matter how difficult it is."

"That's a promise?"

"Yes, Louise. It's a promise."

When the *Try Again* left the dock with the body stowed below, Louise sat huddled in one of the fishing chairs, and it occurred to me as I looked at the fine bone structure of her face that she was going to make a very handsome old lady. Tommy lifted a brown arm in salute and we waved back.

"The party shrinks," Bridget said. "Walk me up the beach a way, Sam'l."

"Pleasure."

"You know," she said, "it makes me think of a cartoon by Abner Dean that I saw a few years ago. It shows these people in a living room, sitting in a circle on the floor with their arms around each other, about eight or ten of them, and they are all sort of melted into each other in a kind of nasty way. They've built a bonfire in the middle on the rug, and the caption says, 'After the others have left, how did we all get so wonderful?' "

"Are we all so wonderful?"

"Maybe I think of the cartoon because we're all so unwonderful. Damn these sandals. Sand comes in the toes."

"What's the matter with us, Dr. Hallowell?"

"Easy question. We're phonies, every one. Those big horrible holes in Warren were reality. And we're so damn far from the realities we weren't really willing to admit that it had happened. It was just a bad line in the script. Hey, Joe, let's shoot this bit over. It don't fit the story line, buddy."

"Who is the phoniest phony?"

"Another easy question. You must want I should win the big jackpot. Guy Brainerd. I lay sleepless on my trundle bed last night and figured him out and why I was attracted to him. You see, he's in the most cynical and potentially dangerous business in the world. Telling people what to think and what to believe. It has been frightening me ever since I've been in it, which isn't long. It's the power that frightens me. There's more power in Manhattan, more power over the human mind, than in any city since the dawn of time. Just suppose, Sam, that every public relations firm, every advertising agency, and every press agent and every columnist joined a concerted effort, a co-ordinated effort to convince the nation that . . . oh, say that everybody is entitled to one homicide a year. They'd sell it, Sam. They'd sell it big. And it would sure cut hell out of the population."

"I can't see Guy as dangerous."

"Oh, but he is! I told you I was uneasy. I felt guilty about the little distortions you feed the public. But, by God, Guy was so sincere about it. I felt he had latched on to some greater truth, some massive justification for what he was doing that far outweighed all my petty little fears. I so needed his reassurance, that I made a transference and told myself I needed him. But you know the truth of the matter? Guy has no special justification. He's just sold himself utterly and completely on the idea that he is doing a Good Thing. He's a shrewd and self-righteous and utterly stupid man. He hasn't a trace of cynicism. He's the high priest of his own mission. And those are the dangerous ones, Sam. Could we please sit on that nice soft rock over there?"

As soon as we sat down she said, "So I'm quitting."

"Why?"

"As a futile gesture, of course. Why else? I'm not going to quit so I can write a great American novel. I'm going to go back to freelance articles and fiction, and do my damndest within my own limitations to keep them honest."

"Can you make out at it?"

"Meagerly."

"So who is phony number two?"

"Mike Dean. The complete cynic. He'd sell his mother's store teeth to buy corn on the cob. Then maybe Bowman, the iron virgin. Cam has sold himself, but he's wryly aware of same. He's the best of the team that I've met. They've got some real horrors on the squad up in New York."

I held my hand out. "Meet another horror, m'am."

She looked at me blankly for a moment, and then looked at me with a contempt that hurt. "Not you, Sam. But now that you mention it, I can see it. It's beginning to show. You sold out."

So I told her how and for how much. I didn't color it. I gave a straight factual report. I told her what would happen. When I was through she didn't speak. She didn't look at me. She got up and walked on up the beach. She didn't walk fast, but she walked steadily until she was out of sight around the point.

If you want a third of a million dollars, there are some things you have to give up.

NINE

So it was Saturday afternoon, and it was hot, and
the breeze was dying, and there were nine of us left
on the island, plus the staff. Nine little Indians. I
sat on my rock and I looked at the empty shore and
I wondered if I should follow Bridget and I decided
it would not do a damn bit of good. Nor would it do
any good to wait there until she passed me on her way
back. I stood up and picked up an empty sun-
white conch shell and threw it out as far as I could.
My shoulder creaked and my arm went slightly dead.
Take me out of the game, coach. I can't put that high
hard one close in against the letters any more. All
I've got left is the slider and the change-up. With
the meat of the batting order coming to the plate.

I walked back to the house. There was just enough
hangover left to make me sweat heavily in the heat.
I kept my eyes nearly closed against the painful
shimmer of light and heat. Amparo Blakely sat alone
at the pool in the shade of an umbrella, reading. I
hesitated and then went to the pool, feeling like a
large unhappy dog that's willing to try anything in
order to get scratched behind the ears. Maybe I
needed that aura of dignity and competence and controlled warmth that she radiated. Or maybe I wanted
to hear some answers without having to ask the questions. She wore a pale gray skirt and a copper colored
blouse that accentuated the coppery glints in her
brown hair. I realized that, of the entire group, when
we had been complete, Cam Duncan, Porter Crown
and Amparo Blakely were the only ones who had never

appeared in swim clothes or sun clothes. I fancied
Amparo would have looked rather well in either.
There was an Amazonian abundance and maturity to
her figure that was emphasized by the narrowness of
her waist.

When I sat opposite her without invitation, she put
her thumb in her book and looked at me through dark
green lenses and smiled.

"Keep on reading," I told her.

"I tried to find something gay, but it just seems
silly."

"Where are the rest of the troops?"

"Resting, I guess. I can't seem to get Warren Dodge
out of my mind. God knows I've seen enough gore.
I've seen them brought in in sickening condition. But
this seemed more terrible. Maybe I'm out of practice.
I've lost my detachment."

"It seems odd for you to have been a nurse."

"Does it?" she asked coolly.

"I don't mean it that way, Amparo. I mean that
once you're a nurse you keep on being a nurse,
usually, or get married or something."

"Are you asking for a personal history, Sam?"

"Hell, I guess I'm just making talk. Now that I'm a
member of the team, maybe I'm just trying to get
acquainted."

"All right. I was a nurse. I had a child, how do they
say it, without benefit of clergy. I could have not had
him, but I wanted him. He's sixteen now, and I visit
him sometimes, and I'm quite certain he has never
recognized me or ever will. I went back to nursing,
but I couldn't make enough to keep myself, and also
keep him out of a state institution. I took secretarial
training. For his sake, I had to be the best, or I'd be
back in the same box. I went with Mike Dean ten
years ago when I was thirty. My son is in a good
private institution. I have a good bit of money laid
away. Any questions?"

"I'm sorry. It wasn't any of my business."

After about ten seconds of silence, she said, "I'm sorry too, Sam. I shouldn't have been so bitchy about it. That thing today upset me. I kept thinking that if I wasn't so rusty, I might have been able to find that artery. And I guess I'm wondering if . . . I wouldn't mean more to myself if I went back to nursing. I loved it, you know."

"What you're doing is meaningless?"

"It's a different kind of meaning. I guess it's like a big gambling game. You put the chips on the right number and you win. And somebody loses. It's Mike's world. I can't picture him in any other kind of world. I'm not being disloyal when I say it's more his world than mine. I mean that I can't ever take it with the same dreadful seriousness he does. Birth and death and pain are the serious things, the meaningful things. We don't have any of those. Except figuratively."

"The pain and death of the Harrison Corporation?"

"If you want to put it that way."

I closed my hand around my leg just above the knee, and felt the hard flesh, the solid meat, and thought of the blood and nerve fibers under the browning skin; and I thought of the way Warren's arm had looked, as if a piece of it had been torn out by a garden trowel.

"Maybe," I said, "I'm having a little current difficulty trying to figure out what the real things are. For me."

"Don't think too much, Sam."

"What do you mean?"

She had an odd expression. "Just think about the rules of the game you'll be in. Don't think about whether the game itself is . . . significant."

"And then I will be able to be very, very happy."

"Cam thinks a little bit too much," she said. "And it makes him restless."

"I'm restless because I feel like a Judas goat."

She looked startled. "That's a phrase Cam uses.

And he smiles that crookedy smile of his and says that they always let the Judas goat out of the pen, because there's always another flock for him to lead."

"It makes me restless."

"And you're being very well paid for feeling restless, Sam. And that's what you want, isn't it?"

I took that little thought back to my room. I lay down with it. And I told myself that wrassling with angels had gone out of fashion. It is a croo-ell world, and you run like hell to stay in the same place, and you get your marks for performance. I would comfort myself with the knowledge that I was still helpful, friendly, courteous, kind, obedient, thrifty, brave, clean and reverent. I could drop the trustworthy and loyal, and after a little while they wouldn't even be missed.

And I knew a hundred guys who would give away their hope of heaven for the chance I had walked into. And grabbed.

Anyway, Mike would keep me so damn busy there would be no thinking time.

And six months from now, Harrison would be a vague memory. There was no reason why I'd ever have to go back. I was going to move in the big time, in fast company. Isn't it the business and the duty of a man to get ahead? Why should I go out of my way to retain the great opportunity of carrying Dolson on my back?

And who the hell was this Bridget Hallowell character to look at me with contempt? She was emotionally unstable. She'd proved she was a pushover. She hadn't grown up yet. She saw things as black and white. When you grow up you know that everything comes in shades of gray. And now, at last, I was all grown up and on my way. With no room or time for baggage like Bridget.

I had built myself a little platform and because it was new it felt slightly tippy, but very soon I would get used to it and stand squarely upon it.

At five-thirty I showered and dressed and headed out to the pool. Bowman was there, and Guy Brainerd and Elda Garry, and Amparo and Bonny Carson and Bundy.

Sometimes I am very unperceptive about social situations. When kicked under a table I have been known to say, "Why are you kicking me?" But it took me only about ten seconds to realize that something drastic had happened just before I arrived. Bonny Carson had an almost hysterical case of the guffaws. Bundy looked like an amused weasel. Amparo was biting her lip and looking worried. Elda Garry was a picture of rigid, outraged indignation. Guy Brainerd had the lost and stricken look of a man who has been unexpectedly disemboweled—and just about the same coloring. Bowman was looking at Guy Brainerd with an expression of icy and concentrated fury that I would not have thought him capable of.

"Scotch on the rocks," I said to John. "Did I miss something, people?"

"If you had half the sense God gave earthworms," Bowman said to Guy, "you would never have brought her down here. You were told that you should assign no one to the Dean account in whom you did not have perfect trust and confidence."

"But I had no idea she . . ."

"That's the point. You had no idea, Brainerd."

Elda said, with a silky venom, "It would be of enormous comfort to all of us, Bonny, if you could stop making that ridiculous noise." Bonny muffled it somewhat, but it did not stop. Elda turned to Bowman. "I'm sure this isn't Guy's fault, Mr. Bowman. But I am certain that I can speak for the editorial staff of *Blend* when I say that if that person goes ahead with what she plans, we should drop this current project."

Bowman studied her for a few moments. "You can't speak for anybody, honey. You can't even speak for yourself. If we decide to go ahead with the Dean story in *Blend,* it will appear in *Blend.* Don't sell yourself the pretty little fiction that you're deciding anything. Before you get rash, just check through all your issues of last year and count the number of pages of advertising from firms in which Mike has a financial interest."

She turned pale and said, "You can't talk to me like this."

"Stay out of the conversation, Miss Garry, or you'll hear some more unpleasant facts."

She jumped up and walked briskly toward the house, bracelets jingling, blond bun bouncing. This time the shorts were rust red, and the pert little rear end managed somehow to express fury and indignation.

Guy jumped up to follow her.

"Hold it!" Bowman said.

Guy stopped and turned and made a helpless gesture and said, "She's very sensitive. You hurt her."

"Then follow her and comfort her." Bowman waited until he had taken two steps and added, "And kiss our contract good-by."

Guy stopped again. He turned and gave Bowman a helpless look. It was unnecessary cruelty, embarrassing to watch. Bowman made him come back and sit down.

"What are you trying to do to me?" Guy said.

"Apparently you want to keep the contract."

"I . . . I'd like to. We've worked together for . . ."

"And now you've pulled a boner that maybe you can't fix. And it will undo any good you may have done in the past. Keep that in mind. And try to figure out just what you're going to do about it. Now you can run along and fondle your lady editor and dry her tears, but don't let it take your mind off the problem."

Guy Brainerd was a fair-sized man, but when he left he seemed to scuttle.

"Wouldn't somebody fill me in?" I asked, as John handed me my drink on a tray.

Bowman seemed to notice me for the first time since I had joined the group. He studied me for a moment, picked up a piece of white paper from the table and turned away, saying, "Come with me, Glidden."

We went to the farthest table, out of earshot of the others. He handed me the piece of white paper. We sat down and I read it. It was neatly typed. The title was centered. THE MIKE DEAN STORY.

Your terribly innocent reporter has just come back from a mad, mad week at the fabulous island hideaway of the mysterious bigshot, Michael Davis Dean. And your reporter is no longer as innocent, and Mike Dean is no longer as mysterious.

Where else, darlings, could a little country girl get such a vivid chance to see the alcoholic and ineffectual husband of the Harrison Corporation heiress get bitten to death by barracuda at the same time that she was contemplating divorce in order to remarry the sterling young executive who had already arranged to sell her pelt to Mike Dean in a secret agreement that will make him rich? Or see a bitter and fading musical comedy star cruelly used as a court jester? Or see how a great big public relations figure sells an idea to a lady editor—between the sheets? Or learn how a rich Texan's pretty daughter amuses herself with the skipper of his private yacht? And much, MUCH more!

But I know this fearless magazine is mad, mad, mad about facts, and so now I shall get down to names and dates and give you the wholesome happy story of my week on Dubloon Cay in the Bahamas. Etc Etc Etc.

I handed it back to him and said, "Bridget, of course."

He folded it and put it in the pocket of his walking shorts.

"Of course. It was very quiet. Guy and Elda and the Hallowell girl were going over the draft of the article. They decided the lead should have more tang. I believe that's the word Miss Garry used. So they sent the Hallowell girl off to whip up a new lead. She was gone about fifteen minutes and came back with this. Guy went right up in the air. So did Elda. She was reading over his shoulder. When they stopped spinning and ran out of breath, the Hallowell girl started in. She made their tantrum seem like a lullaby. She quit, then and there. She used a lot of words for the group. Diseased, sordid, rotted. She's still very young, I think. She said she was going back to freelance work. She said she was delighted to give them the opportunity to read the lead paragraphs to the first article she was going to do. She said she was afraid it would have to go to a pretty gummy sort of magazine, but she had heard they paid very well. You came along about twenty seconds after she left."

"Would it be published? If she wrote it that way?"

"You know damn well it would be published. And it would tip over some very nice apple carts. So we won't let it be published."

"How are you going to do that? Have her killed?"

"Very amusing, Glidden. Very damned funny. It's especially funny when I think of your big mouth."

"Just what the hell do you mean by that?"

"Don't ball your fists, you oversized idiot. I mean that it's perfectly obvious from this piece of paper that she knows you made a deal with Mike. And the only way she could know is if you told her. And since it follows that you told her, then you have an oversized mouth and damn poor judgment. As poor as Guy's."

"Where did all your pretty charm and manners go, Bowman?"

"This is an emergency, and so I haven't got time to pat you on the head, even if I felt like it. You seem to have some influence with the Hallowell person."

"Very damn little."

He shrugged. "You've been sleeping with her."

"How the hell would you know that?"

"It doesn't matter how I know it."

"From Warren Dodge?"

"Stop being so damn trivial! The rooms are bugged. The control panel is in the radio room. It's been handy before, and it will come in handy again. Like the man said, knowledge is power. So I'm electing you to make the first contact with the Hallowell girl."

"What do I threaten to do to her, boss?"

"I hope you're smarter than that. Soothe her. Tell her she lost her temper. Tell her Guy will forgive her and take her back on the payroll with a raise. If Cam was here, I'd let him handle it. He's superb in situations like this."

"So she doesn't listen."

"Then you let her know, as friend to friend, that it will be terribly hard for her to be a successful freelance. Tell her that there could be a few ways that Mike could have her black-listed. And of course, she couldn't ever get back into public relations work."

"And if that doesn't work?"

"Then your tour of duty is over and we put somebody else on the job. Get this through your head. We can't afford to take any chances with this thing. We don't intend to. One way or another, she'll never write or sell that article. This is one of those times when Mike is spread very, very thin. That's one reason why we're handling the Harrison thing our way. He shouldn't have lost his temper with Port Crown.

That makes things just that much tighter. You can start earning your money right now, Glidden."

I knocked at her door. When I knocked the second time she said, "Who is it?"

"Sam."

I heard the key in the lock and then she swung the door open. "Please do come in," she said. "I was making mental book about who they'd send. And it came out you. Big kindly old Sam Glidden, the working girl's pal."

I shut the door behind me. The room was as cheerless as mine. We didn't rate the deluxe accommodations. There was one straight chair by a rear window and she sat in it, looking pale and still and quite drawn.

I sat on the bed and lighted a cigarette and said, "I guess you really tore up the pea patch."

"Be nice and folksy, because that might break me down. When that doesn't work, you can try scaring me. After all, I am one poor frail girl with the whole Dean empire lined up against me. God, they may take away my citizenship."

I wondered if Bowman was in the radio room with the hidden mike in this room turned on. I decided he was. I was a big mouth. I couldn't be trusted. I wondered if he would listen if it were Cam Duncan talking to her. Probably.

Her typewriter was on a small table. I went over to it. "So you did the nasty bit of work on this machine."

"With all my ten little fingers."

I rolled a sheet of paper into the machine and, with two fingers, tapped out, *Hidden mike.* I pulled it out of the machine and said, "Nice type face." I showed her the sheet and as I saw the sudden comprehension, I spoke quickly before she might say anything too revealing, "Your room is just about as enchanting as mine."

"Adequate," she said. "Barely adequate." And she

was looking at the walls, the molding, the corners.

"We might as well talk about your little adventure," I said. "Where do you plan to peddle your new opus?"

"I'll have the exposé magazines bidding against each other for it. If you want to keep up this silly conversation, you can follow me down the beach, but I won't guarantee you'll make any headway. My mind is made up."

We went out the door at the west end of the veranda and down the beach to the left, where she had walked with Louise as an apologist for me, where I had seen them tiny in the distance, one in yellow and one in blue. The sheet I had typed on was crumpled in my hand. When I was out of sight of the house I stopped and dug a hole with my heel and dropped the paper into it and swept the sand over it with the side of my foot. She turned and looked back at me.

"What was that all about? Were you kidding me?"

"Not unless Bowman was kidding me. The joint is wired, he says. And knowledge is power, he says. And before he sent me to soften you up, he let me know that he knows that you and I have been, shall we say, indiscreet."

"Oh, my God!"

"The next step is cameras and infrared and tape recorders, I guess."

"If they haven't got them already." She kicked viciously at a mound of sand. She walked, head bent, hands in the slash pockets of a black denim skirt. "That makes me feel filthy, Sam. It makes me feel all fingerprints. What kind of a routine do they run around here?"

"Happy Mike and his angle boys. Let me get you straight, Bridget. You are going to try to blow up the fun house?"

"I'm not going to try, I'm going to."

"And what do you think Mike will do?"

"Get me on some special sort of black list. Keep me from earning an honest wage. Maybe try some kind of frameup to make me keep my mouth shut."

"But you'll win?"

She looked up at me. "Of course not! I don't expect to. But they're going to have a hell of a fight on their hands."

"Why?"

"Well, there was a book I read. About a man named Charlie who knew he was going to die. And Charlie was up to here with guts. And one of the things he said after he knew he was going to die, and I can't quote it perfectly, but I remember he said it to his wife who had a name I liked. Lael. Charlie said it takes a special man to tell the difference between right and wrong, but any damn fool can tell the difference between good and evil. I don't consider myself on the side of the angels, Sam. But I can fight these stinkers and all their precious rationalizations. And I can fight you too, because maybe you are the worst of the lot."

"Thanks."

"You're perfectly welcome."

"I didn't mean it that way. I meant thanks for blowing your top. It ripped the mask off Bowman. And I got a taste of the future."

"Like it?"

"No. Didn't care for it at all. I've got . . . potentially . . . a hell of a lot more money. And a lot less stature. If he feels like it, he can spit on me. And I have to hold still while he takes aim, because I like the money so much. Then I smile and use my hanky and say, 'Oh, thank you, sir. Any time. Any time at all.'"

"Just so long as you understand it, Sam."

"I know. I counted myself in. And I've been counting my money and telling myself this is a great bunch of boys. But it isn't. So I count myself out."

She took a half step closer to me and had to tilt her head farther back to look up into my face. "Do you mean that?"

"I yielded to temptation, baby. I saw Sam Glidden in the big time. A shrewdie. I saw his pictures in the magazines."

She laughed aloud. "Cliff-sized, slow-moving Sam Glidden, one of Mike Dean's bright young operators, today rumbled that he wants his soul back from the devil."

"Not so much soul as pride, Miss Bridget. I was a pretty nice guy and I didn't realize how much that sort of pleased me. So now I go to Mike and I say look, Mike, all deals are off. I got to get back home and wise up Louise and Tommy and get them onto a proxy deal that will supersede yours. Hope you don't mind, old boy."

"But you signed things."

"And they're all dated June second and I don't get my copies until June second, and if I spend the whole twenty-four hours of June second with some very reliable people watching me every minute, then what good are the agreements?"

"But he can hurt you with them anyway, can't he?"

"Maybe so. But if you're willing to take on the whole shooting match, I ought to be able to at least make a try at it."

"Hallowell and Glidden against the world," she said, and she laughed and she looked very, very good, and I felt very show-off at the moment and pleased with myself; so with one paw on each side of her slim waist I lifted her to kissing height. And when she was up there it didn't require any effort to hold her there, because then her arms were locked around my neck. After a long, long time I put her down.

"I love you, Sam," she said. And then she gulped and put the back of her hand to her mouth and gave me a round-eyed look and finally said, "Where on earth did *that* come from?"

"I like it, wherever it came from. And those three black things on your left leg, and that one black thing on your right elbow, are mosquitoes, because it is now that time of day. Go to the pool and . . . no, go on the veranda, on that settee down near my door, and stay there and be mystic and silent with anybody who wants to talk to you, and I will go cut the tie that binds."

We walked back along the beach and as we neared the dock we heard the clatter and sputter of the little float plane. It landed on the bay and taxied to the end of the dock. Cam Duncan got out onto the float and when the pilot, Bert Buford, swung it tenderly into the right position, he scrambled onto the dock. The plane swung and headed for open water and was airborne before it was completely out of the bay. It headed due west, to the left of the round red sun.

"Everything all arranged?" I asked Cam.

He took his jacket off and hung it over his arm. He looked tired. "It wasn't too bad."

"Are you going to report to Mike right away?"

"Yes, why?"

"Tell Mike and Bowman I'll be in to see them in a few minutes."

He looked at us sharply. "What's up?"

"They'll brief you, Cam."

He went away. We went onto the veranda. We sat side by side. She laced her fingers in mine and said very quietly, "You might as well know, Sam darling, I'm a big bluff. I wouldn't peddle scandal to one of those slimy magazines if I was down to my last dime. I just wanted to scare hell out of everybody."

"And you did. No point in telling them it's bluff, though."

"None at all," she said.

So we sat and held hands for a time and we didn't

have to say a word. It was a very comfortable silence. We watched a fine sunset shaping up, and when I figured they'd had enough time, I left her there and marched to the den of the lions.

TEN

When I went into Mike's room, on invitation, he was in the bathroom with the door open. He was standing in front of the mirror in his rump sprung sarong, shaving with an electric razor. His drink of steaming coffee was on the shelf under the mirror. Bowman and Cam had drinks. Amparo sat with open notebook in her lap, tapping her rather prominent teeth with a yellow pencil.

"How did it go?" Bowman asked.

"She won't play," I said.

"That makes it my turn," Cam said. "This day is too damn full to suit me." He started to move toward the door.

"Don't go yet," I said. "Mike may need you right here."

The buzz of the shaver stopped and Mike came out, coffee in one hand, rubbing his jowls with the other. "What was that, Sam?" he asked, giving me the buddy-buddy smile just as if I hadn't signed anything yet. I could sense the way they lined up, the four of them, alert and canny and suspicious. And very competent. In some crazy way it made me remember when I went to my first dance. The chaperons and the girls had that same ominous flavor of disdain. And, as on that deathless occasion, I felt as though my hands hung too far out of my sleeves, and it seemed grotesque that anybody should have to wear a size thirteen-C shoe.

"I told Cam you might want him around for moral support or something." I sat down, trying to look casual.

Mike slapped his hard brown paunch and said, "You look like you've got a wild hair, Sambo."

"I had a football coach once who called me Sambo and I learned to hate the son of a bitch, Mike."

His mouth tightened. "Let's not get too smart, Sam."

"I'm not too smart. I'm pretty stupid. I let you city slickers sell me down the river. I've got my ticket, but the boat hasn't left yet. So I'm getting out. Right here."

I didn't look at any of the others. I kept my eyes on Mike. There was a long silence. He took a sip of the coffee and set the cup aside. "You are pretty stupid. You're dumber than an ox, Sam. What are your plans?"

I shrugged. "Nothing sensational. I'll go home and get my gang and we'll have a meeting and we'll do a new sales job on Louise and Tommy."

"How much attention," Bowman said, "will the McGanns or the other executives at Harrison pay to you when they find out you've signed up with us?"

"Stay out of this, Fletcher," Mike said sharply. "But you might as well answer his question, Sam."

I scratched my head and hung one leg over the arm of my chair. "Hell, I don't know. All I can do is go back to the way I've always operated all my life, up until now. I'll tell them just what happened. You know, how you people are pretty smooth, and I guess I got a little too impressed by everything."

"Do me the courtesy of dropping that country boy line. Let's get down to business. You think your position is worth a little more than you're getting. You've made a mistake. I don't haggle. You're getting all the traffic will bear right now."

"I'm not smart enough to try anything like that. Bowman did bring up that you're spread pretty thin right now, and I suppose it would be a good time to hold you up. But I'm not doing that."

Mike turned and gave Bowman one long look. Bowman ducked his head and turned chalky.

"So what are you trying to do?" Mike asked me.

"I don't think you'll understand it. I'll put it as simply as I can. I was willing to betray a trust. A hell of a lot of trust from a lot of different people. I thought the money would make up for it. But I've thought about the money for a couple of days and I still feel like a heel. And I don't want to be one of the Dean boys. It isn't my style. I've got the old-fashioned opinion that you people are all sick. So, with fair warning, I'm getting out."

Mike picked up his coffee. I saw that his hand was shaking. "And you do realize, I hope, that your chance of getting a job anywhere after I throw you out of Harrison is going to be just as damn slim as I can make it."

"That's the way the ball seems to bounce."

Mike turned suddenly and hurled the half full cup of coffee into the bathroom. It shattered in the tub. It was, somehow, a shocking gesture. He clamped his powerful hands shut and walked three steps toward me. His face was ugly with anger.

"Why, for the love of God, do I always have to run into this kind of damn nonsense? You were bought and you won't stay bought. What kind of ethics is that? What kind of morality is that? By God, I despise your kind, Glidden. You sicken me. You pollyanna boys want to go around thinking the business world is honorable and reasonably decent. You want to be so stinking noble about everything! Listen to me. There's no more morality or ethics in industry than there is in that pack of barracuda out there, than there is in those barracuda that are digesting chunks of Warren Dodge. You want to live in a dream world. I tell you that the only limitation is the law. And everything else goes. Oh, how I love to run into you Christers on a deal! I don't have to expect any shrewd tricks. Who the hell are you bleeding for? The poor little shareholders? The noble laborer with wife and kiddies? Those sad-pants executives you try to work with?

Maybe the McGanns and the Dodge woman? Jesus!"

"Mike, please," Amparo said, a warning note in her voice.

"Get off my back, honey. I've got to tell this punk. The reason you'll never make it, Glidden, is because you're living in a dream world. You want to be loved. You haven't got the guts to endure being hated."

"You take your dream world, Mike, and I'll stick with mine."

"I'm not in a dream world. I deal with facts."

I stood up. I was seeing things a little more clearly. "You're an emotional cripple, Mike. You're a fat boy locked in the candy store. Some people have compulsive eating habits. You've got compulsive earning habits. You've got to have money, because there isn't another damn thing in the world that means anything to you."

"Do me the courtesy of leaving out the parlor psychiatry," he raved. His face was dark red. "By God, I'll smash you completely!"

"Go ahead. Have a try at it. And Miss Hallowell and I will see just how much harm we can do you."

He followed me toward the door, and he was yelling. I'd stopped paying any attention to what he was saying. It was only when he made a strange sound that I turned and looked at him. He stood holding both hands against his middle. His mouth had a twist of agony. His face had been a tray of coals, but water had been thrown on them and they were wet and gray. He squeezed his eyes shut.

Amparo ran to him. I instinctively took the other arm and we tried to lead him to a chair. He took three steps and went down and I caught him before he hit the floor. I carried him over to the bed.

He groaned when I eased him down. He opened his eyes and mumbled, "Can't see."

"What is it?" Bowman demanded of Amparo. She paid no attention to him. She stared down at Mike in torture.

Suddenly his mouth opened wide. You could see that he was straining for air, but could not breathe. His eyes bulged and the cords in his throat were like the knotted roots of a tree. And very suddenly he stopped straining, and that was all of him. That was all there would ever be. The face was still grotesque.

Amparo's face was ghastly. She murmured something.

"What did you say?" Bowman demanded. "What?"

"Massive coronary occlusion," she said, barely moving her lips. "I saw one before. Long ago."

"He's dead," Cam said softly.

Bowman must have taken a full swing. His fist hit me at an angle of the jaw and I took a chair over with me when I went down. I shook my head to clear it. I moved just in time when he tried to kick me in the face. Even after I had pinned his arms, he tried to slash at me with his teeth. He was like a demented person. "You did it, damn you!" he yelled. "You did it!" Then he went limp, chin on his chest. I moved him three feet and dropped him into a chair.

Amparo had covered the body with a blanket. She started toward the door.

"Where are you going?" Cam demanded.

"I . . . I don't really know."

"We've got to start thinking," Cam said. "We've got to use our heads." But his voice was lost and plaintive. The body of Mike Dean was an oppressive bulk. The spider had died in the center of the web. Amparo sat down quietly. Her face was very still. Tears ran from her quiet eyes.

Bowman slowly pulled himself together. I felt as if, in some curious way, I had rejoined them as conspirator. Bowman looked at Cam. "What will this do?"

"The walls come tumbling down," Cam said.

"I know, I know. Start thinking. I'm trying to." He got up and walked over to the small writing desk, took a zipper portfolio out of the drawer, brought it back to the chair and opened it.

"Status report?" Cam asked. Bowman nodded. Cam went over and stood behind his chair. Bowman took a pencil from his shirt pocket to indicate listings on the status report. "You're in this one, and this one too."

"The timing couldn't be worse," Cam said. "My God, some of them are so delicate that bad publicity like the Hallowell girl has threatened would turn them sour. Now the whole ball of wax goes down the drain —to mix hell out of a metaphor."

"And we're too vulnerable."

"If we had about five days. Even four," Cam said softly. "We could unload. But once this gets out, the bottom is going to fall out of too many things. Those are the things we should dump. Other stuff we can hang onto, like Harrison. It's below book. I'll be damned if I want to lose everything I've picked up in the last few years."

Bowman looked over at Amparo. "Are you in anything current?"

"Just Harrison and Lou-El Drilling."

"The minute it breaks, Lou-El will go down like a dive bomber. Where did you get it?"

"At eight and a quarter," she said.

"It won't level off until it's down to three."

"I've got three thousand shares," she said.

"So," Bowman said, "so you get out with thirty-three thousand right now, or you get out with nine thousand after the news breaks."

"How do I get out right now?" Amparo asked.

Cam's color was better. The mild and engaging smile was not quite back in place, but there was more ease in his manner. "I think that Fletcher and I are thinking along the same lines. It's bad luck Glidden had to be here when it happened, because it would be easier without him. But I think it can be arranged. I can draw up limited powers of attorney for you and Fletcher to sign. And I can fly up to New York and, if we plan it carefully enough, get the three of us off the worst part of the hook."

"When I talk to Ralph Pegler tonight," Bowman said quickly, "I can relay some instructions from Mike that ought to change the picture just enough to make it easier."

"Good idea," Cam said. "I can . . ."

"Hold it, fellows," I said. "Let's back up a little. You want to keep news of his death from leaking out until you can cover yourselves. It sounds like a pretty good trick. How the hell do you expect to work it? I'm leaving tomorrow."

The three of them looked at me. I felt like exhibit A. Or problem A. "There's no reason why you shouldn't give us a break, Sam," Cam Duncan said amiably. "The stuff you signed doesn't mean a thing now. Mike's holdings of Harrison will be tied up in his estate. There won't be any move against Harrison. You'll be free to run the show your own way. I don't think you're going to want to be small about this."

"Small? Hell, you're the lawyer, Cam. There must be some sort of law about withholding the knowledge of death. Why should I get mixed up in your slick tricks by committing a crime of omission?"

Bowman said, his careful charm restored, "Sam, would you mind stepping into the bathroom for a moment and closing the door?"

It seemed childish to refuse, so I went in and closed the door and sat on the edge of the tub. There was a stain of coffee in the tub, and splintered pieces of cup. Mike's razor was on the edge of the sink, cord dangling. I reached over and picked it up curiously, blew the white stubble out of the blades. It was hard to accept that all that vast vitality had been so suddenly stilled. The coronary had killed too big a percentage of the heart muscle, and what was left could not carry on.

I could hear the mumble of their voices. I wished Mike could hear what they were saying. I wondered what he would have thought of it. It wasn't a mumble of prayers for the dead, of lament for Michael Davis

Dean. This was the mumble of money, of sleek and clever avarice. The situation was very much like the way smart operators can sometimes trim a bookie. All you have to do is find out who won the race in time to get a bet down.

Mike Dean, through his considerable powers of persuasion, and through the golden magic of his reputation, and through the clever uses of press agentry, had kept the values of many securities, listed and unlisted, at an artificially inflated value. A lot of speculative investors had formed the habit of riding along with Mike on his raids and ventures. Once the word leaked, there would be a simultaneous dumping of holdings that would skid prices down so fast there would be no takers until the drop leveled off. The sound ones would, of course, climb back to respectable levels. But too many of the companies involved in Mike's plans had been most carefully and legally gutted. Those would go way down and stay way down. Cam, Bowman and Amparo wanted enough time to get out of the building before the roof fell in. I doubted that they would tell any of the New York staff, who very probably were in a similar position. Mike's operating methods weren't of the type to breed loyalty within his own organization.

Bowman opened the door and said, "Okay, Sam." I went out into the room. I could not help glancing at the stillness under the blanket. They seemed unaware of it. They had fresh drinks. Amparo was gone.

"First of all," Cam said, "and I am sorry this part of it has to be so gruesome, I think we can avoid all kickbacks on the time of death. Fletcher tells me that there is one large deep freeze that's not now in use. It's kerosene operated, and it has a lock. Tonight after the staff has gone back to their house, we'll get it operating, and we'll put the body in it. Amparo believes that it will make the actual time of death impossible to detect. The body can be taken out in four days and the death reported."

"That's real nice," I said. Bowman frowned at me.

Cam continued, "I guess you know we've got quite a bit at stake. In return for your co-operation in this matter, I can prepare some ironclad agreements that should give you a return that will be reasonably handsome, but of course nothing like what you would have gotten if you'd gone along with Mike. And he had lived."

"How much?"

"We'll each sign over some of our holdings. They can be predated so as to give you a long-term capital gains. You should clear between twenty and thirty thousand. And you must understand that, in effect, that money is coming out of our pockets."

"Nice big bribe," I said.

"Let's stay clear of the ugly words. We'll all be more comfortable," Cam said. "We'll all go to New York tomorrow. Just Fletcher and Amparo and the staff will be left here. You do not say a word of what happened to anyone. I'll help you liquidate what we sign over to you. Then you can be on your way."

"What's the alternative?"

"You stay on the island until I'm damn ready to let you leave, any of you," Bowman said, his face ugly.

"That would be a pretty good trick, too."

"Not as difficult as you might think."

I stood up. "And not as easy as you might think."

"Are you going to be difficult?" Cam asked plaintively.

"Sure am," I said. "I don't want any piece of this thing. If you boys are caught in a bind, it's because you had your necks out, and that's too bad. But you're both sharp, and Amparo is a good secretary, so you shouldn't be hurt beyond repair. I think that my people at Harrison should know about this just as soon as possible. And I'm going to let them know just as soon as I possibly can."

I expected them to try to block me at the door. But they let me go. Bowman gave me a cold and savage smile as I looked back at them. He lifted his glass. "Good luck," he said.

And it was forty minutes before I learned about the hole card, the ace that had made them so calm. Forty minutes, before I guessed why Amparo had left while I was in the bathroom.

There wasn't much light left in the west when I got back to the dark veranda where I had left Bridget. She was tense and slightly indignant. "What took you so *long*?"

And I told her. It shocked her terribly—not only Mike's death, but their plans to save themselves.

"I thought Bowman was a nasty piece of work," she said, "but I sort of liked Cam and Amparo. But they're just like Bowman, aren't they?"

"In their own way. The words may be different, but it's the same tune. So we've got to get off the island."

"How?" she asked.

"Why, by boat, I guess."

"Indeed?" she said sweetly. I looked down at the dock. The *Try Again* was gone. The three skiffs were still tied up.

"I saw Romeo down there about ten minutes ago," she said. "He fiddled around for a while and I couldn't see what he was doing, and then he took off like a bat."

So we went down to the dock. Nobody seemed to notice us, or care. The outboard motors were on the rack in the dock house. We batted at the mosquitoes that whined around us. The housings were off the sides of the motors. I knew without further investigation that some essential parts were gone, and those parts would be on the *Try Again*.

My Bridget had asked a helluva good question. How?

She whispered, "How are you at swimming?"

"Not that good."

"I was making a joke. Why are we whispering?"

"I don't know. Let's get away from the bugs."

We went back up to the house at a half run.

"What's the point?" Bridget asked.

"I won't play their game, so they won't let us off the island. None of us. So it doesn't matter if you and I and Guy and Elda and Bonny and Bundy do know he's dead. They'll have a way of getting Cam off. So they keep us right here until Cam gets the three of them healthy up in New York. Then what do we do? Sue? I have a hunch they'll come out of it with enough money to buy their way out of any jam that might arise because of this."

A few moments later, in a dreamy voice, Bridget said, "I never in my life have seen a house party go more completely to hell."

ELEVEN

DINNER ON SATURDAY NIGHT was a strange occasion. For the first time since my arrival, the food was indifferently prepared and carelessly served. Amparo, Bowman and Cam did not put in an appearance. Quite obviously the staff was badly rattled. There were just the six of us. Booty served us at a table in the lounge. She banged the dishes down in a great hurry, and didn't hear you when you spoke to her. Her eyes were enormous. Dinner was quite late—late enough so that Bonny Carson got well loaded beforehand—and when it was finally served, the main course was tepid.

I had told them about the sudden death of Mike Dean.

I had expected Guy Brainerd to be utterly crushed. But in a most curious way it seemed to hearten him. His big jaw become more firm. "In effect, Glidden, it solves a problem for me. Elda and I talked it over this afternoon. Even though the annual fee he has been paying Brainerd Associates is handsome, there comes a time when a man must weigh profit against . . . his personal pride in himself and his work. I had about made up my mind to cancel the Dean contract."

"And I told Guy," Elda said, "that a man of his standing should not have to endure rudeness."

Bridget made an almost inaudible and entirely disrespectful sound. Elda Garry stared at her furiously. "After all Guy has done for you, you should be ashamed of yourself, Miss Hallowell."

"But think of what I did for both of you!" Bridget said and winked broadly at her. The lady editor turned red in the face and stabbed her fork into a piece of the overdone and cooling roast.

Bonny frowned into space and said in her deeply husky and blurred voice, "Figure he's going to walk in any minute. Never thought they could kill Mike. He was all man. Mean as a damn snake, but all man. You gotta give him that."

"I give him nothing, nothing at all," Bundy said shrilly.

Bonny turned her head slowly and looked at Bundy with a certain almost regal dignity. "You know, sometimes, Bundy, you're a nasty little jerk."

"So okay! But what did he ever do for us?"

"He was a great guy." She crossed herself quickly and then began to cry and, a few moments later, left the table, stumbling over the sill as she went out onto the veranda.

Bundy stood up and patted his mouth with his napkin. "You got to excuse her," he said. "It's just temperament. You know, she's sentimental like. All great artists are that way. You gotta know how to handle them."

He trotted after her.

"That dreary little type is almost touching," Elda said. "He seems so terribly devoted."

"Oh, he's terribly devoted," Bridget said, smiling at Elda. "Bonny's last two agents dropped her because they couldn't see any future in handling her. So now she's with poor little Bundy and she's the only client he's got who ever made more than two hundred a week, and he's got one chance of making a dollar out of her, so he's extremely touching and devoted. I think it's so charming the way you can sentimentalize everything, honey."

Elda dropped all her Manhattan mannerisms and bawled, in pure Iowa, "Get off my back!"

Guy said heavily, "I hardly think this is the proper time for quarreling, ladies. Remember, we're all in the same boat. To put it bluntly, if Mr. Glidden is

correct, we're being held here against our will by unscrupulous, and if I may use an old-fashioned word,
wicked people. And we will be here for several more
days, it would seem. I have important matters in New
York that I should attend to. I think we should give
our attention to seeing if we can think of some way
out of our . . . dilemma."

"If you want to do any planning," I said, "don't
do it aloud either here or in any of the bedrooms. The
whole joint is wired, and apparently Bowman is the
one who has been doing the most listening."

I saw Elda and Guy give each other a look in which
horror and shame were commingled. His bald head
turned as dark and moist as a pickled beet. And she
turned so pale she looked greenish. She swallowed
with an effort.

"Are you absolutely positive?" Guy asked me.

"Almost completely certain."

He banged his fork down. "Had I known that Mike
Dean would lend himself to any such . . ."

"Chicanery?" Bridget said helpfully.

"Chicanery, I would never have accepted a public
relations contract. There is one thing I have always
said. I must be able to believe in the man, the idea
or the product that I am . . ."

"Standing behind of?" Bridget suggested.

He gave her an annoyed glance. "Yes. Yes, of
course. I do not care to deceive the public. But,
obviously, Mike Dean was deceiving me. I valued him
as a friend. I was not aware of his . . ."

"Multifarious deceptions?" Bridget said in a honeyed voice.

Guy jumped up, glared down at her, and walked
away.

"Why do you insist on being so unpleasant to him?"
Elda asked.

Bridget muffled a yawn. "Oh, I donno, kid. Maybe
it's because I recently found out he's the most in-
curable stuffed shirt in all the wide world."

"He's a wonderful and charming man!" Elda said hotly.

"Defend him, kiddo. Stand up for him. I just can't . . ."

And every light went out. Elda gasped. Bridget found my hand and squeezed and said, hollowly, "And she knew that there in the darkness, perhaps inches from her dainty ankle, the dread mamba lay coiled to strike."

"Stop it! Please!" Elda said. "Oh, Guy! Guy!"

"Coming, darling," he said, and I heard him blunder into a chair and curse under his breath. He felt of my shoulder and said he was sorry and worked his way around the table.

Booty came into the room carrying two candles. "Generator broke," she said, and put one candle on the table and went away with the other, her shadow vast and wavery.

It was a half hour before the lights came on again. By then it was after ten. A wind had arisen, again out of the northeast. When Guy and Elda said good night, Bridget and I went down onto the dock. Out at the end it was clear of mosquitoes.

"To think I thought I was in love with a type like Guy," she said.

"Instead of a type like me."

"Don't get fatuous, Glidden. Get practical. Get us off the island. Get us off now. I've got a crazy idea. I've got the idea somebody is going to kill somebody. I don't want it to be you."

"We can untie a skiff and paddle with our hands and, hell, Grand Bahama is only thirty something miles over that-a-way some place."

"One of those skiffs has oarlocks, Sam."

"The hell you say! Which one?"

"The smallest. But there aren't any oars."

I climbed down into the smallest to check, and found out she was right. I went back to her. Something was niggling at the back of my mind. A pair of green oars. But where? I told her to stay right there. I went into the dock house. My lighter flame flickered. The oars stood in a corner. I left them there.

I went back to her. "Oars," I said. "But it's thirty miles!"

"More than thirty miles, and the wind will be some help if it holds in that direction, and you are a great big boy now, and besides, I can spell you. So go get . . ."

I clapped my hand lightly over her mouth, and turned her head so that she too could see the figure standing quietly in the faint moonlight at the end of the dock.

So we talked maybe too gaily of other things until it went away. Whoever it was, mosquitoes didn't seem to bother it.

"We can figure on three miles an hour and be conservative," I said.

"Call it eleven hours, then," she said.

"And take into account getting lost and getting swamped and getting blisters and so on and so on."

"But, brother, wouldn't it scare hell out of them!"

"Are you trying to shame me into it?"

"You're going to try it, Sam, aren't you? I know you are. I can tell from your voice."

"Okay, okay. Shall we go pack?"

She hugged my arm. "I'm a silly and temperamental and emotional woman. And I want to leave right now. I don't want to go near that house."

It was a crazy gesture, but she had an infectious and persuasive way about her. And there was something too real about her fear.

With utmost caution I got the oars and made certain they fitted the oarlocks. She got into the stern. I untied the line. The oarlocks squeaked and I dipped the pins in the water and they stopped. I took long, strong strokes, and tried to be as silent as I could be. There were two lights on in the house.

She was silhouetted against them. The house dwindled, but with an uncomfortable slowness.

We left the bay and turned southwest toward the point. She kept turning and looking back. After a time we could no longer see any lights, but we still whispered.

After I had rounded the point and the wind was behind us, I rested on the oars while I checked the constellations in the night sky and, using the island as a reference point, I set a clumsy course to follow.

"Want me to row now?" she whispered.

"We can use a normal tone of voice now, Murph."

"Stick with Bridget, huh? Do I row?"

"When I get tired. Off we go. It's about eleven." I made the oars bend and made water gurgle against the bow. The oar handles overlapped in an annoying way, and every once in a while I would bang my knuckles. After a time I found a comfortable rhythm. Bridget sang about bell bottom trousers, her voice a clear and true contralto in the night. She knew all the words. Then we made up some more words. We were enormously gay. It was a lark.

Until the moon went under; soon after the stars were gone, and the wind freshened, and the first wave broke over the stern and she had to begin to bail with her cupped hands because there wasn't anything else. Then it was not at all gay. We were tiny people in a tiny boat on a turbulent and immeasurable sea, under the dark vault of an alien and endless night. What had been partially a lark became a damn fool venture, serious and deadly.

We had to talk loudly to hear each other over the sound of the wind and the cresting water.

"Are you staying ahead of it?" I asked her.

"I . . . I think so. I can't see very well. And I keep getting slivers."

By looking astern I could see the white froth of a breaking wave in barely enough time, each time, to avoid the worst of it by giving a hard pull at the oars.

"What did you say?" I asked her.

"I said I keep wondering what I'm doing here."

A good question. What the hell were we doing out in a fourteen-foot flat-bottomed skiff in the middle of the night with no idea of direction? I was thoroughly scared, with good reason. I hoped she wouldn't crack up. I suspected she wouldn't.

"This is what they call the cruel sea," she said. And I knew then she would not break.

I pulled until my shoulders ached and my arms were leaden. Then came a hard rain, hissing across the sea, sounding like a train bearing down on us. The hard rain flattened the sea, and gave her a chance to get ahead of the incoming water. In the flashes of oddly blue lightning I could see her clearly, blond hair pasted to the shape of her skull.

But after the rain the wind became stronger and the waves broke more often, and I knew we couldn't survive long in a following sea. As soon as I sensed that we were in a period of relatively quiet water, I turned the boat as quickly as I could. We took some over the side, but not seriously. I held it with the bow into the wind. I could not have rowed much longer. My palms were greasy with blood. Salt water had gotten into the broken blisters. The motion of the skiff was more violent, but we were not shipping water. Bridget worked with stubborn and desperate energy and finally stopped.

"The pumps are staying ahead of the battle damage, Captain, sir."

"Good work! Go below and get yourself some hot chow."

"Aye aye, sir. Any idea of where we are?"

"Not the slightest. We should be on course."

"If the wind hasn't shifted."

"If the wind hasn't shifted. Right."

It took a long time before I was breathing more easily, and a longer time for the pain in my side to go away. The fragile moon reappeared between clouds. We were in a silvery wilderness, lifting high on the polished gunmetal waves, dipping heavily into the troughs. Every now and again a wave would break near by, with a hissing, sighing sound, and the foam would be swept off into the darkness astern. The moon disappeared, and when it came out again briefly, I saw that Bridget was leaning over the transom, being ill.

"Are you all right?"

"I haven't got my sea legs yet, Captain, sir."

"You're relieved. Go to your stateroom."

Without warning another sheet of the hard warm rain swept across us. It rained so hard that it seemed to make it impossible to think clearly or breathe properly. When it ended, Bridget was bailing again, throwing a pathetically small amount of water over the side each time she made the scooping motion with her cupped hands.

And the first wave broke over the bow. I cursed my stupidity and, as soon as I had a chance, I kicked one shoe off and tossed it to her to use for bailing. I got around onto another seat so that I would push with the oars rather than pull, and so I could see the water ahead of the bow.

I do not know when I decided that it was most probable that we would not live through the night. I know it was some hours later. The wind was increasing steadily. It was only by the greatest of luck and a new skill, painfully acquired, that I kept the breaking waves from swamping us. But I was becoming far too weary. My reflexes were slowing. I knew how it would happen. Two or three waves would fill us and I would be unable to prevent the unwieldy boat from turning parallel with the waves, and then one would roll us. We would cling to the boat until we could cling no longer. And very soon after that we would drown. And I did not care to drown. There was too much ahead. And she was curiously included in all of it.

I saw one coming and I could not move in time. It half filled the skiff. Another one right now would do it. But, as though by a miracle, the water seemed more calm. The wind had not lessened. But the water was not cresting and breaking. I could not understand it. And then I heard a surf roar that seemed far away. And I understood the calmer water. The wind had drifted us by an island or a reef and we were partially in the lee of the obstruction. I turned around and nearly lost an oar in my haste. I pulled toward the sound. The water became more calm. And the wind seemed to decrease. Soon it was as calm as in the bay at Dubloon Cay.

"What's happened?" Bridget demanded. Her voice sounded unnaturally loud.

I rowed until I felt an oar scrape bottom, and then with two final rocking, straining strokes, I drove the skiff aground and slumped over the oars, the breath tearing in my throat, my heart beating like a thick and hasty drum. My hands felt as if I would never be able to straighten my fingers.

"Sam!" she cried. I lifted my head. The moon had come out again, and the sky was much more clear. We were twenty feet from a crescent of white beach jeweled by moonlight. The dark brush began beyond the sand. The island seemed small and narrow. If the wind had not changed, we were on the southwest side of the island.

I wedged my foot into the sodden shoe and stepped over the side of the boat. The earth was wonderfully solid and safe and stable. I held her hand while she stepped out and, still hand in hand, we walked to the beach.

After two steps on the sand, she broke into forty pieces. She sagged against my chest, gulping and sobbing and whinnying. It was reaction, I knew, and it made her gallantry during the black hours more touching, and more commendable. These, I knew, are the rare spirits of the world, the ones who stand up to anything that can be thrown at them, and save the quakes until the danger is over.

Just as she began to pull herself together, we were assailed by ten billion hungry bugs. They had jaws and stingers and blood thirst. We did some wild, flap-armed dancing, and we went out into the shallow water but they followed along, a keening savage cloud around us.

"Windward side!" I yelled at her.

We ripped and flapped and danced our way through the tugging fingers of the brush and came out on the far side not over fifty yards away. Fifteen feet beyond the brush the wind was so strong we could lean against it, and we were magically free of sharp assault.

In the moonlight I saw, fifty yards to my left, a half acre jumble of the familiar black rock of the islands. We walked through the wind and through little gusts of salt spray to find shelter among the rocks. Though it was a warm night, I realized I was shivering. Part of it was the wind against the soaked clothing, and part of it was exhaustion.

Bridget, with the prehistoric instincts of the Neanderthal cave wife, found a sandy hollow in the lee of a five-foot shelf of rock. It was about eight feet long and four feet wide. The moon was in such a position that we were in the moon shadow of the big rock. I heard her teeth chittering. We were in our special place of warmth and protection. The wind whined, but could not touch us.

"Get out of those wet clothes and into . . ."

"If," she said, "you should say dry martini, I might hit you with that rock. That big one. The clothes are coming off."

We undressed. She insisted on being the little homemaker. She stood up and spread the damp clothes out on the lower shelf of rock to the left of me. She piled small stones on them so they wouldn't blow away. She worked with her back to me. Her legs, halfway up the thighs, were in the black pool of shadow. Her hair was platinum. Her tan back was a tawny ivory. Her buttocks were purest marble. She was the loveliest vision I had ever seen. I owned the island and the sky and the hemisphere. Then she came down out of the wind and stretched out beside me. The sand and the rocks were still warm from the sun of the day that had ended so long ago. I reached for her, and pulled her close, and kissed the side of her nose, and found a pillow for myself on that precious softness that is equally distant from point of breast, point of shoulder and point of small determined chin.

And as I felt the first stirrings of a great need for her, I lost my balance and missed a frantic grab at the last of consciousness, and slid backward and upside down—down the long steep velvety chute that dropped me into a sleep almost as deep as Mike's. Or Warren's.

TWELVE

I woke up flat on my back and opened my eyes and glared up at a deep blue sky that glared right back. Something small bounced off my bare chest and I recognized it as the same sort of thing that had awakened me.

"Cut it out!" I mumbled.

"Oh, such a nice sweet-tempered man in the morning. I'm so glad I found out in time."

I opened my eyes again and turned my head and looked at her. She sat crosslegged in the sunshine atop the ledge of rock where she had put the clothes out to dry. She had a handful of small pebbles. She plunked another one off my chest. She was fully dressed. My clothes were folded and neatly piled in the approximate order I would put them on. Her hair was a tangly mop, slightly damp.

"Good morning," I growled. I realized I was buck naked. I sat up.

"Good morning, darling. I've been up a long time. I've done all the housework, and I've drawn you a nice warm tub. Right out there." She pointed toward the water. "I've had my bath."

I got up and trudged woodenly into the ocean. The water was clear and I kept a careful watch on the bottom. When I was up to my waist, I plunged and wallowed and floundered. I made seal noises and dipped sand off the bottom and scrubbed myself. My hands stung like fire. They looked in worse condition than they were.

She was gone when I came out. I dried quickly in the sun and the early morning breeze. I dressed in

dry wrinkled clothing, a little crusty with dried salt.
The prints of her bare feet were in the wet sand
near the water. I followed the trail to the other side
of the island. Halfway around I saw the house. It was
weatherbeaten, deserted. There were broken boards
in the porch.

I found Bridget staring at an empty cove.

She turned to me and said, "Dearest, I'm afraid
somebody stole the car right out of the garage last
night."

"I have true and classic intelligence. I am a very
sharp citizen."

"Did you leave the keys in it, dear?"

"There was an anchor and an anchor line, and all
I had to do was remember that there are tides in
the ocean. And drop the anchor over the side."

"Do you like your eggs sunnyside-up or easy-over,
dear?"

I walked to a palm pod and sat down. She came
over and sat beside me. "I'll be serious for two or
three seconds," she said. "I can't find anything I'd
risk trying to eat, and I can't find any water. And I
tried your lighter and it is finished. So it is going to
be a very good idea to wish real hard for a nice boat
to come by, I think."

"I think so too."

"I'm not going to get scared."

"I know you won't, Murph." So I kissed her, because that seemed indicated, and then we did some
exploring on our island, and learned to stay away
from the shrubbery where the bugs lived. The sun
climbed higher and hotter. We could see four other
islands. Off to the southwest the sea looked empty.
But it was so vividly streaked that we knew we were
still in the Bahama Flats. At an estimated ten o'clock
we saw a fast boat about three miles away, heading north.

I peeled the sodden cards and sticky money out of
my wallet and put them in the sun to dry. Remem-

bering something I had read, I dug a hole just above the high-tide mark. I used my hands and a stick and a hefty piece of shell. After I got down over two feet, water began to seep into the bottom of it. I dipped some up with a shell and tasted it. It was warm, brackish and thoroughly nasty. I was thirsty, but not that thirsty. Yet I suspected that it would keep us alive.

Bridget had the idea about the empty whisky bottle. There was a fine supply of same in and around the ruined house. We gathered a little pile of dry leaves and small twigs. By experimentation we found the right way to hold the bottle in the sun so that a tiny white-hot spot was focused on a brown leaf. It took time and patience before it began to char and smoke. I huffed at it until I was dizzy, and finally we had a fire. I went out into the water and found some fat conchs and brought them in. We smashed the shells, removed the creatures, pounded them between rocks with the hope it might tenderize them, and then cooked them over our fire, impaled on green sticks we had broken off.

We said they were just fine. They were edible. Barely. The sun was overhead, and then it began to slide toward the west. I did not care very much for the idea of another night on the island. If there was no wind, we would be eaten alive.

"Well now!" Bridget said. I looked at her. She was staring at a coconut palm.

"Trust us to overlook the obvious," I said.

We considered the problem. I could get up the palm and I could get them down. But how do you tell which ones you want?

"I think they slosh, sort of," Bridget said.

"And how do you open them?"

"That's easy," she said. "I've done it a dozen times. You sit on your back porch with a hammer and a big nail and you hammer the nail into a special little place on the end of it, and then you pour the milk into a jelly glass."

"Of course," I said.

At the expense of several square inches of hide, I got up the most promising tree, twisted the nuts loose and dropped them. I split and scraped the husks off on the rocks and used a conch shell to pry a rusty nail out of the house. I hammered it straight between two rocks. I pounded it into a coconut, then worked it out. I poured her a shell full of the cloudy liquid. She drank it and held out her shell and said, "More."

"Fix the fire first, woman. It's going to go out."

She fixed it. We drank the juice. She sighed and said. "Look at us! Water, of sorts. Fire and food and fruit juice. Sam'l, I've got a funny idea about us."

"What is it?"

"I think we can survive, no matter where they drop us. I think we can make out."

"Is this a proposal?"

"For goodness sake, don't leer like that."

"Okay, but look. I'm a fool for work. I work a twenty-hour day when I have to. You could get lonely sometimes."

"I'm a woman of resource. I've got scads of fertile ancestors. So I'll fill our tarpaper shack with a raunchy crew of little Gliddens, all with runny noses. When the bill collectors come, they'll say mommy is out in the shed writing a novel."

"Please don't look over your left shoulder, Murph, or you'll see something coming so directly at us that all I can see is the bow wave on either side of the white bow."

It was an eighteen-foot open boat from the Grand Bahama Club, one of the charter boats. It had twin outboards. It had a brown little guide named Spider. It had been chartered for the afternoon by a couple from Indiana named George and Kate Thatcher. It had an ice chest and, on the ice, several bottles of an English brew called Dog's Head Ale. Nothing had ever tasted quite as good. They told us it was quarter to four. They had caught some Spanish mackerel and some small amberjack trolling, and Spider had suggested running over to the island and trolling for some barracuda before going in. And we said that was very, very lucky indeed. Kate was worried about George's sunburn, and she was willing that we should run right back in. It was only nine miles, Spider said. About thirty minutes with five in the boat. I went and collected my dry money.

As Spider was pushing us off the shallows, Mrs. Thatcher said incredulously, "You were *rowing?*"

"Sure," Bridget said. "You know. A little moonlight row on Saturday night."

"And you spent the whole night on the island?"

"Well, about half of it. We got here pretty late."

But by then Spider was ready to roll, and the roar of the motors made all further conversation impossible. I looked at my blonde with the tangled hair and the ruined clothes, and she looked very good indeed. At the Grand Bahama Club dock we thanked the Thatchers and Spider, warm and heartfelt thanks. Bridget and I walked up to the hotel, and through the lobby, trying not to notice the people who stopped in mid-sentence to stare. We went out the far door and acquired an ancient and asthmatic Chevy which took us down to the village and waited for us in the muddy yard of the tiny cable office.

I sent one to Al Dolson. MIKE DEAN DIED HEART ATTACK YESTERDAY. ALTER PROGRAM ACCORDINGLY. BACK SOONEST.

And Bridget sent two. One was to a friend on a New York paper, a managing editor. WILL DICKER ON EXCLUSIVE ON YESTERDAY'S DEATH MIKE DEAN AT BAHAMA HIDEAWAY. FELLED BY CORONARY AMID BIG DEALS.

She handed the second one to me instead of to the man. It was to her folks. PLAN MARRY KING-

SIZE CASTAWAY. BELIEVE CAN CIVILIZE IN
TIME. DETAILS FOLLOW.

She raised one calm and questioning eyebrow.

I handed the cable blank to the man, and we held
hands in the rackety cab all the way back to the
hotel.

I had a very lucid idea of what was going to happen, of course. I would go back to Portston and find
time to be married, and then put in a few years of
hard labor turning Harrison healthy.

I did go back and we did get married on the
Fourth of July, and we did find out that it was going
to be the very best of marriages. You never know
that until you try it a while.

Harrison was in no danger from the remnants of
the Dean organization. The empire fell apart completely, and very quickly. Bridget and I had given
it the final push, and we were not sorry. I did some
checking when I was in New York and found out that
Amparo had gone back to nursing, Cam had gone
back to his home town and into private practice,
Fletcher Bowman was still looking.

Bonny Carson's musical opened in early December. And closed in early December.

Louise lived alone in the big house, terribly
muted and terribly tragic. Tommy and Puss sold
their house and moved to Texas.

So it should have gone the way I thought it would
go. But the Harrison Corporation was still a crippled
animal in the jungle, and we couldn't move fast
enough. I had a year of it before a crew that called
themselves Kell-Mar Associates moved in on us.
They'd picked up the Harrison holdings from the Dean
estate. The operation was headed by a little man
named Kellison. He wanted to engineer a merger because our loss picture made us damn attractive, tax-
wise, to one of the more profitable firms in the in-

dustry. At least it was slightly more wholesome than the raid Mike Dean had planned.

We put up a battle, but maybe by then we were getting a little weary of battles. And Louise and Tommy were bored with trying to sustain old and meaningless loyalties.

So it went through. And they cleared us out. Me and Dolson and Budler and Murchison and the rest.

I had plenty of places I could go. And be placed fast. But I wanted time to unwind, and get the world back in perspective. So I listed myself with an executive placement agency in New York, and after we counted our money, I said I would be available on January first.

And so right now we are taking our long delayed honeymoon in Mexico, and we have a small house with a walled garden and a tiny swimming pool and a beaming maid named Carlotta and a morose and effective gardener named Miguel.

I am on the patio, in the shade. On the table at my right is half of a tall rum drink. Beside the drink is the most recent report from the agency. And this time I like the sound of the job and the size of the salary. And the idea of living in San Francisco. When dusk comes I will have a committee meeting with my Bridget and we will make a decision, maybe.

I needed this time to unwind, and get reacquainted with myself. And my bride. We have often talked about the lurid week on Dubloon Cay. It was not a waste. It gave me a clue to myself. It taught me that under certain conditions I could become a rascal, and readily rationalize my own rascality. Bridget says that will keep me from becoming too fatuously pleased with myself. She says every man should be aware of his own capacities for villainy, so he knows what to look out for.

From where I sit I can look out into the sunny garden, at a picture I admire. I look through a fringe of flowers at a green pool, and beyond it a gray wall heavy with flame vine. And above the wall, a deep blue sky.

Bridget is between the pool and the wall, supine on the faded yellow canvas of a poolside cot, her forearm across her eyes. In the privacy of our walled garden I have no objection to her wearing the startling bikinis she adores. No objection at all. This one is fashioned of red silk bandannas, and the Mexican sun has browned her most beautifully.

It is quiet in our Cuernavaca garden, and I run a loving glance from high instep up straight leg to convex thigh, up to red silk breasts and gentle throat and round firm chin.

She insists that it is beginning to show, but I cannot see it yet. But the timing will be fine. Around the end of March a new Glidden will take its first angry look at a dazzling world.

I look at her and I think of my crazy luck, and it makes my eyes sting. And I have the superstitious fear that something will spoil it. But if something wants to come along and spoil it, it will first have the chore of killing Sam Glidden, inch by inch.

So I go out into the garden on the pretext of seeing if she needs new ice. But actually just to be closer to her.

THE END
of a Gold Medal Novel by
John D. MacDonald

SUSPENSE...
ADVENTURE...
MYSTERY...

John D. MacDonald's
TRAVIS McGEE SERIES